Air Ryder

(Harper's Mountains, Book 3)

T. S. JOYCE

Air Ryder

ISBN-13: 978-1533595782
ISBN-10: 153359578X
Copyright © 2016, T. S. Joyce
First electronic publication: May 2016

T. S. Joyce
www. tsjoyce.com

All Rights Are Reserved. No part of this book may be used or reproduced in any manner whatsoever without written permission, except in the case of brief quotations embodied in critical articles and reviews. The unauthorized reproduction or distribution of this copyrighted work is illegal. No part of this book may be scanned, uploaded or distributed via the Internet or any other means, electronic or print, without the author's permission.

NOTE FROM THE AUTHOR:

This book is a work of fiction. The names, characters, places, and incidents are products of the writer's imagination or have been used fictitiously and are not to be construed as real. Any resemblance to persons, living or dead, actual events, locale or organizations is entirely coincidental. The author does not have any control over and does not assume any responsibility for third-party websites or their content.

Published in the United States of America

First digital publication: May 2016
First print publication: June 2016

Editing: Corinne DeMaagd
Cover Photography: Furious Fotog
Cover Model: Caylan Hughes

DEDICATION

For the 1010 Crew.

My fellow foul-mouthed, dirty-minded,
hilarious weirdos.
Your shenanigans are my happy place.

ACKNOWLEDGMENTS

I couldn't write these books without my amazing team behind me. A huge thanks to Corinne DeMaagd, for helping me to polish my books, and for being an amazing and supportive friend. And to my man and our two cubs, who put up with a lot of crazy work hours from me and take everything in stride. I won't turn into a total mushpot right now, but my little family inspires me and keeps me going in so many more ways than they even know.

And last but never least, thank you, awesome reader. You have done more for me and my stories than I can even explain on this teeny page. You found my books, and ran with them, and every share, review, and comment makes release days so incredibly special to me. 1010 is magic and so are you.

PROLOGUE

Ryder gritted his teeth and chucked the chair as hard as he could against the wall of the trailer. It shattered into a thousand splinters over the old shredded couch. He fucking hated this. He fucking hated everything.

His insides were molten, and every muscle was filled with adrenaline that made it impossible to stay still. She'd ended it. Ended them. Ended him.

One stupid text had ruined his life. A text! He'd loved Erica with everything he had and she'd broken up with him via *text*?

He shoved over an old table and kicked viciously at the debris on the floor.

This is what Clinton did when he got filled with

too much emotion. He came into the Trash Trailer and destroyed shit. Right now, Ryder was so mad his inner owl wouldn't even come out.

Ryder threw a vase against the wall, but it didn't ease the hurt in his chest. He squatted down, overwhelmed that nothing was helping. Hands gripping the back of his neck, he screamed as loud as he could.

"Boy, what are you doin'?" Clinton asked from the doorway.

"What you do when you're pissed."

The crunch of Clinton's boots on glass was loud in the quiet of the trailer. He lifted Ryder by the neck of the shirt and shoved him roughly into the only chair Ryder hadn't destroyed. Then the tall, dirty blond, bearded Crazy Clinton leaned his back against a dresser he'd stripped the drawers from and crossed his arms over his chest. "I know what this is about."

"You don't know nothin'," Ryder argued.

"Boy, talk to me like that again, and I'll whoop your ass."

Ryder believed it, too, so like the wise owl he was, he zipped his lips.

"I've watched you act out for years now," Clinton

murmured, eyes narrowed, head cocked. "You got somethin' deep in you that you can't fill. I know that feeling."

"She was it for me."

"Erica wasn't it. She liked the idea of dating a shifter, didn't matter who it was."

"I mattered!"

"Not like you should've. Trust me. She ain't it."

Ryder huffed a humorless breath and nudged the jagged shards of the vase that had scattered across the floor with the toe of his boot. He shook his head in denial.

"You're eighteen—"

"You bonded when you were a kid."

"Yeah, and it almost broke me! Why do you want a bond so fucking bad right now, kid? Huh? It's hard. It fills your head. I mean shit, live a little before you tether yourself to someone else. Find yourself. Make yourself good enough to care for a mate before you go trying to force a bond."

More crunching glass, and now Ryder's stepdad, Mason, was standing in the doorway. "Erica?" he asked in that deep tenor that should've soothed Ryder, but right now it only made him feel like his feathers had been ruffled the wrong way. He didn't want Mason or mom worrying.

"She ended it with me. I'm fine." Ryder murmured.

"You aren't." Mason squatted near Clinton, his dark eyes earnest. He turned a splintered table leg over and over in his hand like he was mulling over what he wanted to say. "Just because this didn't work out doesn't mean you fell short."

"It does."

"It doesn't, Ryder. You have it in your head that you aren't enough, and boy, I swear you are."

"Not for Erica. Not for…" His real dad. That asshole was the one who put the hole in his middle in the first place. No one could fix it. No one could fix him. "I want what you and Mom have," Ryder admitted low to Mason. "I want someone to see me and want me as much as I want them. I want to take care of them. I want kids. I want happy ever after."

"But you're not there yet," Mason said softly. "You're young, Ryder. You haven't met her, but someday you will."

"When?"

Mason shook his head. "I don't know."

"Beaston told me he couldn't see my mate."

"Beaston don't see everything," Clinton muttered. "That don't mean you won't find one."

"I just have this feeling that I'm going to be one of those bachelor shifters who won't be able to bond to a mate. I won't be able to get it to stick."

Mason stood and sauntered over to him, pulled his head against his side, and clapped his back roughly. "Air Ryder, you got me to stick with a look. From the first time I saw you, you were my boy. You're enough."

Ryder relaxed against the man who had come into his life and become his father, no questions asked. The fire in his middle cooled, and he squeezed his eyes tightly closed. Mason had given him everything—a home, a place in the Boarlander Crew. He made Mom happy.

So why the hell did Ryder still feel so wild?

"You want to go piss off the roof and set somethin' on fire?" Clinton asked.

Ryder let off a single, soft laugh and nodded. "Yeah."

He stood and gave Mason a rough hug, then ducked out of the way when he ruffled his hair.

"Maybe you'll get the girl next time," Mason said.

Ryder turned at the door and offered the man who'd raised him a slight smile so he wouldn't worry. "Maybe so."

God, did he hope. He couldn't even imagine the pain of being a ship at sea forever without finding his anchor.

ONE

Alexis Porter pushed open the door to Alana's Coffee & Sweets and hoped to hell Alana still had some of her cherry turnovers left. Alexis's clients had been very specific. She was to cook everything for their breakfast in the morning except the turnovers Alana Warren's café was known for. Those they wanted imported from Bryson City.

There was no one behind the counter, but a quick look around and Alana was standing at a booth in the corner, arms locked against the bright lime green table. She was talking low to a redheaded man who was staring out the big front window with his hands linked behind his head. Freckles covered his face, and his eyes were a strange color she couldn't identify from here. Looking pissed, he shook his head at something Alana said.

She shouldn't be staring, so Alexis forced her gaze away from him and made her way to the counter.

"I'm serious, Ryder," Alana said, as the sound of her shoes thudded across the wood floors. "Don't let her do it."

Alana was shaking her head as she ducked behind the counter, her chestnut curls twitching with the gesture. She looked up with a smile, but her soft brown eyes were troubled. "Hey, Lexi. What can I do for you?"

"Uuuh, please tell me you have cherry turnovers left. I know I'm late in the day, but my clients won't be moved on these."

Alana put up a finger and ducked into the kitchen, then back. "Do you have ten minutes to wait? They'll be fresh out of the oven."

"Oh my gosh, you're a life saver."

Alana giggled and said, "You might as well add them to your menu. What is that, three requests in two weeks?"

"Yeah, you're killin' me. Thirty minutes each way

every time a client does this."

"Dayum," she said through a grin. "I still can't believe my café has taken off like this since the remodel. It gave me a platform to advertise my pastries." Alana leaned onto the counter and lowered her voice. "I think by the end of this month, I might actually be able to pay my bills *and* pay the deposits for the wedding."

Her dark skin practically glowed in the afternoon sunlight that streamed through the front window. That glow had shown up after she'd met her fiancé, Aaron, a few months back. It was good to see love do that to someone Alexis had known for so long. But the second Alana's eyes flickered to the table in the corner, her smile disappeared.

Alexis followed her worried gaze. "What's wrong?"

Alana heaved a sigh, blowing one of her curls out of her face. "That one over there doesn't know when to let go. If you're gonna sit down while you wait, I would suggest anywhere but by him. He's an emotional monster on Tuesday afternoons."

"Okay," Alexis murmured.

Alana bustled off into the kitchen. Alexis looked

around at the full tables and the only two open were a booth next to the redheaded muscle man or a table in front of his. Great. She debated just standing here like a dope for the next ten minutes, but customers were filing in the door, and she was in the way.

Slowly, quietly, she padded to the booth and sat down. When the man looked up at her for an instant, she was stunned by his eye color. Gold irises, red hair, all those muscles stretching his thin T-shirt and, holy sheeyit, they didn't make 'em like this around here. He must've been an import to Bryson City. She would've remembered him.

The man cracked his knuckles and glared down at his closed laptop sitting on the table in front of him. He checked his watch, stared at it for ten seconds, blew out three quick breaths, and opened the computer.

His sensual lips thinned into a plastered smile as he leaned back on the bench seat and sat still as a robot. "Come on, come on, come on," he murmured through his teeth. His brightly colored eyes narrowed to slits as time went on, and he muttered, "Come on you jerky-shirted sucker-puppy—heeeey." The forced smile was back. "There you are. You actually answered this time. Hey Serena, you look great." He looked like he was about to barf on those words.

If Alexis strained, she could just hear the voice on the other end of the video chat he was on. "Can't say the same for you, Ryder. You look like shit without me."

Alexis gasped as her cheeks heated to fire. What a little she-demon. Embarrassed to be eavesdropping, Alexis looked anywhere but at the man. She couldn't leave now, though, or it would be awkward. Shoot. *Come on turnovers. Cook faster!*

Ryder cleared his throat and leaned forward, lowered his voice. "Can I talk to her?"

"She doesn't want to talk to you because you left her. You left her, you left me, and we're both pretty fed up with how you ended everything."

Whoa, he left his kid behind?

"First off," he growled out, "I left you, not her, and if we're being technical about it, you really bowed out when I caught you sucking on Stewart's micro-penis in our bedroom. And furthermore, I still can't believe you fucking left me for someone named *Stewart*."

"He's an accountant with a steady income. What

do you do, Ryder? Nothing. You sit around and get drunk with your friends and talk about all these babies you want but can't provide for."

Ryder waved his fists around in a furious little tantrum. "Just let me see her! You don't have to strip me down, Serena. I just want to see her. Just…let me see my baby."

"I'm breeding her soon."

Breeding her? What the fuck?

Ryder's mouth fell open, and he shook his head slowly. "Don't say that."

"I'm breeding her, and you'll never see her puppies."

Oooh, thank God. They were talking about a dog, not a child.

"You're a terrible person," Ryder whisper-screamed. "Those will be my grand-puppies! I want her back—"

"You'll never get her back until you come home."

"I am home."

"Home is where I am! You said I was it. You bonded to me, so Stewart shouldn't have changed your feelings."

"I saw you lick his hairy balls."

"So? You're an animal, Ryder. You could've fucked around with other women, and I wouldn't have gone to such an extreme. You moved across the damn country."

"His O-face was so gross looking." Ryder's lips were twisted down like he wanted to retch. He made an appalling, ridiculous face with his mouth hanging open wide and moaned a couple times. "It was like that. Do you really want your kids to have faces like that?"

When he made the face again, Alexis snorted, then pursed her lips against her laugh.

"No, because I don't want kids, like I've told you a billion times."

"False. You told me it one time after we'd been together for three years and after I had to clean Stewart's nut-sweat off my bed sheets. Stewart looks like a pimple and smells like hamster farts."

Alexis nonchalantly put her hand over her mouth to hide her laughter and looked behind her so Ryder wouldn't see her face. But nope. She couldn't stop her shoulders from shaking with her silent laughter.

"Are you done?" the woman asked.

"Ryder," Alana warned from behind the counter.

"Finesse, or you won't get what you want."

Alexis peeked back just as Ryder inhaled deeply, his muscular pecs pressing against his T-shirt that she could now read. *Blow me, it's my birthday*. Geez.

"Does he snuggle Dottie when he's watching television?" Ryder asked. "Hmm? Does he take her to the dog park and on walks? Does he buy her new collars and share his ice cream cones with her? Does he wipe her mouth after she eats?"

"Oh, my God, no, because she's a dog, not a baby."

"She was *my* baby."

"And now she's mine. If you want to see her so badly, then come back."

"Bark, bark."

Ryder's ruddy brows lifted high, and he looked so hopeful. "Dottie? Dot, come here, baby. Come in front of the camera!" He squinted. "No, don't let mommy push that button. Bite mommy!" There was some kind of scuffle, loud static, and now Ryder was grasping the screen in a death grip. "Don't!" The sound cut off, and he stared at the screen with eyes the size of dinner plates.

Ryder stood and yelled the word, "Noooo." He gripped the edge of his computer like he would flip it, but Alana reminded him blandly, "You need that."

In one smooth motion, Ryder picked up his mug and raised it in the air to throw it on the floor.

"Break that dish, and I'm gonna tan your hide," Alana said.

Ryder set the mug down gently, ripped open a sugar packet, and moved to pour it on the floor when Alana said, "I *know* you won't."

Looking utterly pissed, Ryder sat down and dumped creamer into his coffee, then crumpled up the small plastic container in his fist, and all the while he glared at Alana, daring her to say something.

"She makes me so mad," Ryder gritted out. "I should call her back."

"No!" Alexis and Alana yelled at the same time.

Ryder jolted upright, eyes locked on Alexis as though he'd just now noticed she was here. The restaurant had grown eerily quiet as she froze under his attention.

Clearing her throat, Alexis said, "Speaking from a female point of view, if that little...jerky-shirted sucker-puppy hung up on you just to avoid letting you get a glimpse of Dottie, she's drama. And she's probably sitting by her computer waiting for you to call so she can feel superior. She likes the power she has over you right now. Don't give her that."

"But my dog—"

"You need to let her go. That woman uses the dog as leverage."

Suspiciously, he asked, "How do you know so much about girls?"

"My vagina is my resume." What in creation had just possessed her to say that?

"Your turnovers are ready," Alana called.

Perfect timing. "It was nice to eavesdrop on you," Alexis said. "I mean meet you. You're very cute." *Stop talking.* "I mean, I like gingers." *Just leave.* "I mean you can do better than that nut-licking floozy." She stood and looked heavenward for the strength to stop rambling. With a tiny wave at the striking man, she muttered, "Bye bye now," like a total dork, and then hurriedly shuffled over to the counter where Alana was ringing up her box of pastries.

Her fingers shook as she rushed to pay, and she told Alana to keep the change just to escape faster.

"What's your name?" Ryder asked from across the room.

"Uuuh, Alexis. People call me Lexi."

"Sexy Lexi, I like it."

Alana rolled her eyes and handed Lexi the bag. "Ryder, don't be a twat."

"That doesn't offend me. I love twats."

Lexi snorted, but swallowed it down and bit her bottom lip to hide her smile. This man was too amusing for his own good, or hers. "Bye, Alana." She gave her friend a polite smile and high-kneed it for the door.

"See ya later, Sexy Lexi," Ryder said. But where she expected to see humor on his face, his eyebrows were drawn down and furrowed.

He was so cute! Those freckles and fair skin, perfect nose, great smile, dimples, and now his eye color had morphed to a vibrant blue. He was definitely one of those shifters, but she had no clue what kind. For all Lexi knew, he could be a bear shifter like Alana was now.

She forced herself to break her gaze from Ryder's, and just as she did, she smashed face first into the glass door. Mortified, she apologized—to the door—then escaped out into the sunlight. She inhaled deeply as she jogged to her mud-splattered black jeep parked right in front of the café.

As she pulled out of the parking spot, she looked through the window of Alana's shop one last time to see Ryder standing there, head cocked, eyes narrowed as he watched her leave. He was biting the corner of his lip like she was as confusing to him as he was to her.

He was taller and wider in the shoulders than she'd been able to tell before, and now her hormones were surging. It was probably just the animal in him that was affecting her like this. That was a thing, right? She'd seen it on websites. Animal magnetism or something.

Yeah. That was all it was.

Lexi hit the gas and blasted down Main Street and away from the sexy, red-headed giant. The sooner she got back to work up in the Smoky Mountains, the better. That man was hung up on his ex, and Lexi had been there, done that.

She would not set herself up to be any man's rebound.

TWO

Weston muttered a curse as he poked and prodded at the undercarriage of the four-wheeler he'd flipped on its side. "Doesn't make any sense, man. It should start."

"It's electrical," Ryder said from where he sat on the back porch stairs of their connected cabins.

"It's not. I already checked."

"It's the switch."

"Goddammit, Ryder, it's not the switch."

Ryder shrugged and went back to rubbing his thumb across the inside of his palm and thinking about *her*. Sexy Lexi. She'd taken up his entire headspace since yesterday, but he couldn't figure out why. Maybe it was how frazzled she'd seemed when he'd talked to her, or maybe it was the sexy way her full lips formed the word *vagina*. Hell, maybe he was just curious about why she'd bolted from the café. Nah, it wasn't curiosity. It was those big ol' titties popping out from her camo-printed tank top. Camo on top, a push-up bra, obviously, little jean shorts hugging that juicy ass of hers, and hiking boots that made her legs look like they needed to be wrapped around him as soon as possible. It wasn't just her curves that had him drawn up when she'd told him not to call Serena back though. It was her face too, or more specifically, her eyes. They were a strange color between green and amber. Mood eyes maybe. They probably changed colors when she was pissed. So fuckin' sexy on a human. And her hair? Jet black and long, soft curls stretching down over those perfect jugs of hers. Dark tresses paired with all that mascara shit on her long lashes made the green-brown of her eyes pop even more.

She'd stunned him. Even more surprising? She'd stunned his owl.

That probably meant it was about time to get laid again. Serena drove him crazy every fuckin' Tuesday and made him desperate to snuff his ex out of his mind. And this week, Ryder's inner bird had just happened to land his horny sights on Sexy Lexi.

His best friend, Weston, pulled the four-wheeler back upright and shoved a couple of probes on the wires coming off the starter switch. He turned it on, but his machine didn't make a single solitary beep.

"Told you," Ryder gloated.

"Dang," Weston said, standing back to glare at it. "We ain't got the part for that."

"I'll order it tomorrow."

Wes wiped his greasy hands on a rag that used to be white but was now the color of soot, then frowned over his shoulder at Ryder. "Are you gonna tell me about the call yesterday or not?"

"You already know how it went, psychic."

"Don't call me that. I haven't had a single vision about you or Serena. You *told me so* about the switch, but I *told you so* for three fuckin' years about her." Weston squatted and started poking around near the throttle before he murmured to himself, "That woman is a little monster in human skin."

"Yeah, well, she was my little monster."

"Bullshit, she was never yours. She cheated on you, then took your dog and all your money, man. She made you into a damn country song. You open yourself up too much in relationships."

Ryder gritted his teeth against verbally reaming Wes and shook his head, staring off into the early spring woods behind the double cabin. Wes didn't get it. He'd never needed anyone else. Not really. He was strong on his own, but Ryder had been wanting a bond with a mate since he was a kid. He really thought he'd found it with Serena.

Wes would only give him a hard time, though, so he kept that little gem to himself.

To avoid the hell out of this conversation, Ryder said, "I applied for the permits to use the land behind Harper's Mountains to make trails. We also got the LLC paperwork back. Big Flight ATV Tours is officially ours."

"Alana said you've been asking her about some townie named Alexis Porter."

"Alana has a big mouth and is being a terrible second best friend," Ryder muttered grumpily. He was definitely going to burn a dick shape into her and Aaron's front yard tonight.

"You gonna ask her out?" Wes asked innocently.

"You gonna give me shit about it?"

"No. I think it's a good idea. Alana thinks Alexis is single. Plus, you have Serena up on this pedestal, and you need to put yourself out there and literally take any other person in the world out on a date to see she wasn't that awesome."

Ryder frowned suspiciously at the back of Wes's head as he worked. "I thought you said bonds were stupid."

"Yeah, they are. Sex isn't stupid, though, and you need your dick stroked. Your ego, too. You talk a big game, have a sarcastic comment for everything, but I've seen you at Drat's. You won't even get a girl's number anymore. Serena shook you up."

"No, she shook up Stewart the accountant. P.S. we need Wi-Fi out here ASAP. It super-sucks having to make my weekly call to Serena in Alana's café. I'm pretty sure I'm drawing the crowd on Tuesdays so the town can watch my chronic emasculation. I came this close to seeing Dottie today." He squished his finger and thumb together. "*This* close."

"You need to let that dog go, man."

"Yeah, that's what Sexy Lexi said, too."

Wes snorted. "I like her already. Logical, thinks with her head, not her heart. I approve."

Ryder picked up a stick off the porch and chucked it at him. "You know, bein' heartless ain't all it's cracked up to be."

Wes stood and leveled him with a green-eyed glance. "And how did that break up feel, Ryder? How does it still feel?"

Ryder ducked his gaze and refused to answer, but Wes wouldn't be ignored.

"Huh? How does it feel?"

"Feels like she ripped my insides out," Ryder admitted low. "Feels like I'm walking around empty."

"Because you let her walk all over you, man. You completely ignored all the bad shit she was doing to you. Next girl, take your time, go in easy, just have some fun instead of thinking she's *the one*. Guys like us aren't meant to pair up like that."

"What does that mean?"

"We're flight shifters! We don't bond like bears, boars, or gorilla shifters. We can't Turn a human. We don't give claiming marks. We're basically humans with the ability to shift into animals. Nothing more."

"You can't really believe that."

"I do. And the sooner you realize it, the sooner you'll see you're searching for something that doesn't exist. How can you ever be happy if you don't learn to be content with what you have?"

Weston turned around and went back to fiddling with the switch on the four-wheeler. Ryder scrubbed his hand down his short facial scruff. Maybe Weston was right. Maybe Ryder needed to stop searching for a mate and just accept it wasn't his destiny. It wasn't his fate to have this epic love story like Harper and Wyatt, like Alana and Aaron. Maybe Beaston had given the prophesy that he and Weston would be friends—blood brothers—for always because he knew there would be no mate bond for either of them.

Fucking Stewart with his tiny penis and fucking Serena for wasting three years of his life with her lies. She'd sworn up and down she felt a bond with him, but she didn't even know what love was. Hell, he obviously didn't know what a bond was supposed to feel like either.

Maybe Wes was right, and Ryder just needed a casual sex-capade to get him out of this funk.

Chasing Sexy Lexi's fine ass would be the perfect distraction.

THREE

Lexi snapped the lid closed on the last plastic container of leftovers and set it with the others in the fridge. She liked this cabin's kitchen most. Out of all of the high-end rustic properties Smoky Mountain Paradise Cabins owned, this was the biggest and most expensive for clients to rent. The kitchen was sprawling. Shining granite countertops gleamed in gray with dark speckles and veins of black shimmer, and the cabinets had been stained a rich walnut color. The appliances were new and stainless steel, and the stove had six burners instead of the four the other cabins had.

Her clients, Mr. and Mrs. Randal, had been awesome to serve. They'd emailed her the exact menu a month in advance and reserved her personal chef services for four meals of their seven-day stay. They'd chatted cordially in the hot tub on the back deck as she'd prepared the hors d'oeuvres, and they'd giggled like newlyweds during the four-course meal she served them.

They were here celebrating their twenty-fifth wedding anniversary, and Lexi had admired them all through dinner as their laughter echoed around the house. She wanted that. Someday.

Perhaps not right now when she was reeling from what Blake had done, but someday she wanted to fall head over heels in love with someone who only had eyes for her.

She cleaned the kitchen, packed her extra supplies in her tote bags, and then she brought the half-empty bottle of chilled white wine out to the back deck where the lovebirds were enjoying a game of checkers in the shade.

The view out here always astonished her. The cabin was on stilts and sat high up in the air overlooking a gently rolling river with thick greenery all around. The forest was coming to life after a long winter. This was her favorite part of the year, when the Smokies bloomed.

"Lexi, everything was wonderful," Mrs. Randal gushed.

She grinned and topped off their wine glasses. "Well, I appreciate it. You have been a pleasure to serve. Is there anything you need from town?"

"The concierge said you do grocery runs," Mr. Randal said with a slight frown at the checker board. His wife was smoking him.

"I do, and I would be happy to pick the groceries up and deliver them in the morning if you would like. The service will be charged to the card you reserved the cabin with."

"Perfect," Mrs. Randal said with a beaming smile. "That way we can hole up here and not have to go all the way to Bryson City tonight. There is a grocery list and your tip on the dining table."

With a slight bow of her head, Lexi murmured, "Thanks so much. I'll leave my number on the counter. Feel free to call at any time if you need to make a change to your grocery list, or your menu."

She said her farewells, collected the list and her tip, then made her way outside where her Jeep was parked near the Randal's rental car.

Lexi was dressed in her professional best, wearing her official chef outfit assigned to her by the owner of Smoky Mountain Paradise Cabins. Her Jeep, however, was a study in opposites. It sat on giant mud tires with black rims and had a rooster tail of dirt down both sides. She'd actually had to wipe grit off her lights last night just so they would illuminate better, but getting around to all these backroad cabins was muddy business in the spring.

Movement caught her eye in the woods, but when she jerked her attention to the trees, there was nothing there. Just gently swaying branches. As she stood there frozen, the hairs prickled on the back of her neck. She rubbed the gooseflesh there and hurriedly shoved all of her things into the back of her ride.

But when she turned around, the movement was back. She gasped. A massive white owl sat on a thick branch of a towering oak tree. The owl seemed abnormally large, and when it stretched out one of its wings, the long, perfect feathers were speckled with a chocolate brown. The sound of its long, curved talons against the bark sent shivers up her spine. The owl was beautiful, but didn't seem natural out here in these woods.

In a rush, Lexi bolted around to the driver's side and yanked open the door. When she was inside, she locked the doors, as if the bird could lift door handles or something. She knew her fear was irrational, but that didn't change the adrenaline dump happening inside of her body right now.

Her hands shook as she jammed the key at the ignition, missed, and tried again with success. Blowing out a breath, she pulled around to the dirt road that led out of here and blasted past the tree with the mutant owl. When she looked up into the branches, its head was turning slowly, its eyes tracking her escape. So creepy.

Maybe she should call animal control. That thing was big enough to eat her dog, Sprinkles, in one gulp. The Randals hadn't brought pets, but some of the other clients at the cabins had.

Okay, but there were black bears in the area, and a slew of other predators, and that was the risk clients took bringing their animals out into the woods. They even signed waivers that the cabin rental company wasn't liable for any pet accidents. Would being eaten by an abnormally giant owl count as an accident?

After she put a few miles of distance between her and the bird, Lexi relaxed enough to turn up the radio to one of the only stations that came through out here. An upbeat country song came on, and she hummed along off-key. It helped to settle her.

The forest blurred by as she hit the main road that would take her home. Feeling a hundred times better, she sang louder, making up words where she didn't remember them.

Up ahead, off to the side of the road, a man stood with his leg propped up on a log. He was shirtless, clad in only low slung jean shorts that were a dozen inches too short. As she slowed down, the man poured a plastic gallon jug of water over his bright red hair and rubbed the water all over his rippling abs in slow motion.

Her Wrangler rocked to a stop. Slowly, she rolled down the window. "Ryder?"

"Take a picture."

"What?"

"Take a picture for your spank bank."

He picked up another gallon of water and dumped it seductively over his chest.

"How many jugs of water do you have?"

"Just take the picture!"

"Okay." She pulled her phone from the cup holder and lifted it slowly. *Click*. Well, if she ignored the fact that she could almost see the head of his pecker hanging from the short shorts, he did look good with all those muscles.

Ryder shook out his hair like a dog, then sauntered over to her jeep like he was on a fashion runway and threw open her passenger side door.

"No, wait!" she said, holding up her hands.

Ryder sat down with a squish and grinned at her, his eyebrow cocked. "How was that for you?"

"Where is your car?" she asked, looking around. The road was empty.

"I flew here."

"You...flew?" Realization hit her in an instant, and she freaked out, kicked open her door, and bolted outside. "You're that giant owl?"

Ryder held his hands out as though he was confused by her abrupt exit. He got out and leaned on the hood of her ride. With a naughty grin, he pointed to his dick and said, "Yeah. *Giant* owl. I thought about doing a naked scene for you, but then I thought maybe nah, my giant dong can be intimidating at first glance, and I think we should be friends before we get to the benefit part. I mean, I don't *really* think that because I'm a dude and would be fine if you wanted to do benefits now, but I read a book about how you have to seduce women slowly, so..." He frowned. "What are you wearing? No matter." He gestured to his lap. "You still gave me a boner."

Lexi shook her head hard to rattle her churning thoughts into a coherent sentence. "So you planned this...photo shoot? For me? Like, you put jugs of water out here, and those shorts are on purpose?"

Ryder scrunched up his face in a cocky-male expression and said, "Yeah."

Lexi scratched her head and murmured, "Okay, I'm going to go home now."

"Cool. Do you want me to ride with you or follow behind? I can fly, but I'll be losing the shorts, and when I Change back, I'll be bare-ass naked. The choice is yours."

"No, you aren't coming home with me."

He offered her an utterly offended frown. "Wait no. I have questions."

"What questions?"

He pulled a small notebook from his back pocket and slung water off of it before he held up the first scribbled page for her to see. "Interview questions. I'm shopping for a third best friend."

"Friends," she said suspiciously.

"With benefits who like to pet each other's—"

Lexi shook her head in warning, so Ryder amended, "Friends who are just friends."

Better. Lexi rubbed her hand over her forehead and looked around. With a sigh, she gestured to his notepad. "Okay, ask me."

"Number one. On a scale of one to ten, how much do you like giving blow jobs to—"

"Ryder."

"So a ten," he murmured, making a note.

Lexi pursed her lips against her smile because he didn't need encouragement.

"Number two. Do you like dogs?"

Good, a normal question. "Yes."

"Three. What percentage of time do you spend in the mornings on choosing lingerie versus the clothes you wear?"

She gave him a dead-eyed look.

"Fine, pass. Four, multiple choice. Do you want

seven, eight, or twelve children?"

She refused to answer that one, too, but now it was getting harder not to laugh, and Ryder wasn't helping because he wasn't keeping a straight face either. She rested her fingertips nonchalantly over her lips to hide the smile there.

"Five..." He cracked a smile, then smoothed back out his face and tried again. "Five, what cup-size are your tits?"

Okay, now that she knew this was a big joke to him, she wanted to play. "I'm a B-Cup."

Ryder ticked his mouth in mock-disappointment and jotted down some notes.

"But," she joked, "they swell to full Cs when I'm on my period."

"Mmm," he said, fighting a grin. "I've never been so excited about a woman's menses before."

He stood there staring at her, his eyes dancing with the smile he was trying to stave off, and she couldn't do it. Couldn't hold his gaze, or she would lose it. She stared off into the woods and clenched her teeth against the laughter that was bubbling up her throat.

"I have questions for you now," she said.

"I'm an open book and have no shame. Hit me."

"Where did you find those tiny shorts?"

"Someone from my old crew showed me how to make them out of jeans."

"Great, how did you find me?"

The ghost of the smile dipped from his lips. "I asked around about you."

"From Alana?"

"No." He narrowed his eyes. "Yes, but she wouldn't dish any dirt, which is pretty shitty of a second best friend."

"So I would be your best friend after Alana?"

"Yeah," he said, as if the answer should've been obvious. "We hardly know each other. I found you on the Internet."

"You mean you stalked me."

"Whoa, whoa, whoa, lady," he said, holding up his hands. "I didn't stalk you. I just tracked down your job, where you would be working today, and the road…you…take home." He frowned. "It's not weird until you say it out loud."

"Well, you didn't have to go to the trouble because I planned on stopping by Alana's café on Tuesday to watch the train wreck that is your love life and possibly sit with you to offer my support while your ex reams you."

His answering grin was stunning. His freckles stood out against his pale skin, his eyes were a bright and beautiful blue color, and dimples sank into his cheeks as his smile lines deepened. It didn't help her hormones that he was shirtless and his nipples had tightened to sexy little bitable buds right now.

She was staring. When she forced her eyes back up to Ryder's, he had the cockiest smile she'd ever seen on a man's lips. Shaking her head, she prepared to make her exit because this man was trouble with a capital T. "It's been nice chatting with you, but I have to get home."

"Say no more."

Good, at least he got the hint. But when Ryder slid back into the passenger's seat, she leaned on her open window and shook her head in exasperation. "Out."

"When should I pick you up for our first friend-date then?"

Lexi narrowed her eyes at him, but Ryder only relaxed back and rested his feet on her dashboard, and now his muscular butt-cheeks were hanging out of the shorts. Ridiculous man. Sexy, yes, but ridiculous first. Why did she find his behavior so amusing? She'd always been one to date serious types. But this wasn't dating. It was just friendship with a funny guy who made her laugh.

"How about you drop by my booth during Taste of Bryson City on Saturday morning? I'll be giving out samples of food in a purple tent near the middle of Main Street. You can hang out with me there if you want."

"Done. I will do that for you," Ryder said, sliding out of her Jeep. He strode around the vehicle, and she expected him to jog back across the street to retrieve his plastic pitchers, but instead he sauntered straight up to her and wrapped his arms around her.

Lexi froze, shocked to her bones.

Ryder tensed when their torsos met. He huffed a small breath as though surprised, too, then gently rested his cheek against her temple. Gads, he was tall, and so strong against her. She should balk at hugging a complete stranger but after Blake, it felt so good to have a man willingly touch her. Slowly, Lexi wrapped her arms around his waist and relaxed against him. She didn't know how long they stood there like that on the side of the road, just hugging, but after a while, she wanted to cry for some reason she couldn't understand or explain.

Ryder was a goofball and liked to joke around, but this was a different side. A softer side that pleasantly surprised her.

He moved his cheek slightly, and she could've sworn he kissed her there on her hairline, just a silent peck before he eased back. She thought he would have on a silly smile like he'd been wearing before, but he looked down at her with an intense, almost confused, expression on his face.

"I'll see you Saturday," he murmured in a deep, rich timbre that sent warmth streaking down into her middle.

"See you," she whispered.

And then Ryder opened her door for her, waited for her to get in, never taking his eyes from her, and shut the door beside her gently. He opened his mouth to say something, but closed it again and patted her open window twice before he pushed off and waited for her to leave.

As she drove away, she looked into her rearview mirror at the confounding man who was shaking up butterflies in her stomach that she never thought she would feel again. Ryder stood on the side of the road with his hands linked behind that fiery red head of his, watching her leave with a frown etched into his face.

She understood that look because one glance in the mirror at herself, and she wore the same one. She was baffled by him, too.

FOUR

Lexi was being ridiculous. An hour into the Taste of Bryson City event, and she had already convinced herself Ryder wasn't coming. Did that stop her from scanning the crowd every millisecond like a hopeful nutjob? No.

Across Main Street and up a few tents, the Bryson City Fire Department was cooking hamburgers and hot dogs on a giant grill with a buffet table set up with all the condiments. And one Aaron Keller was standing as greeter, talking cordially to passersby. From the Internet stalking she'd done on Ryder's crew, he was one of the Bloodrunners. Second to Harper Keller, the dragon alpha herself. Never in a million years had Lexi thought one of the rare dragon shifters would end up here in tiny town, North Carolina. And Kane didn't count. No one had actually seen the dragon inside the quiet man with the terrifyingly green reptilian eyes. Two tents down was a green one with Alana's Coffee & Sweets logo on the front banner, and Alana was serving small plastic cups with samples of her pastries. She caught Lexi's eye and waved.

Lexi flipped the shaved steak on the griddle quick and waved with her tongs.

Alana was part of Ryder's crew, too, the mate of Aaron Keller, so where the hell was Ryder? Or should she say Air Ryder, because that's the name apparently everyone in the whole world knew him as. She'd never kept up with shifter culture, but he had a *huge* following. Lexi's Internet stalking had told her that Air Ryder was a badass rare shifter with personality for days, and one of the most famous flight shifters in the entire world. And the more of his posts she'd read, the more attention she noticed from his online followers, the less sense it made that he was showing interest in her. Who was she? No one special. Just a small town chef who enjoyed a quiet life and didn't know the first thing about shifters or

Air Ryder's culture.

This was probably a game to him—chasing her, getting her crushing hard on him, then dropping her. Just the thought sent another ache through her stomach. She'd barely eaten in two days, all because she had been so nervous for today. It was just a casual meeting of new, sort-of friends, but she couldn't shake the happy feeling that had warmed her when she'd stood on the side of the road in his arms.

For the first time in years, she'd felt safe, and okay.

Lexi slapped a slice of cheese to melt on top of the steak and stirred the mushrooms she was sautéing in a giant pan on another griddle.

Behind her, Sprinkles whined. She was leashed to one of the legs of the tent, which she hated. Her little back legs lay limply to the side, her tail completely still, but if Sprinkles was able, she'd be wagging at Lexi right now for looking at her. Sprinkles was paralyzed on her back end, but that hadn't slowed her down at all. Once Lexi strapped her into her tiny wheels, Sprinkles loved to run and didn't stop until she was worn out completely.

"Sorry, baby. Today is gonna be a little boring, but we'll go on a big walk when we get home."

Sprinkles, clearly pouting, lowered her chest to the pink, bejeweled dog bed and heaved a sigh as she looked up at Lexi with the saddest expression in her giant eyes. God, the little Chihuahua slayed her. Lexi giggled and went back to making the miniature Philly cheesesteaks. There was a line forming, and there were only three samples left on the table, so she hurried to make more.

For the next half an hour, she was blissfully too busy to dwell on the fact that the funny redhead she had a teeny crush on was standing her up.

Table full of samples and the crowd dwindling momentarily, she inhaled all the delicious scents filling the air and rested her hands on her aching lower back. She loved this town. Sure, it had the same problems every small town had, like everyone knowing everyone else's business, but the people were friendly, and were helpful when a member of the community got into a jam.

Couples and trios and chatting families walked this way and that, but when she looked up the street to check on the line at the Fire Department's hamburger station, a flash of red captured her attention.

Ryder was walking away from her, but abruptly he stopped and strode deliberately toward her tent. His eyes on the asphalt, he seemed to be talking to himself as he ran his hand roughly over his head.

When he looked up and locked eyes with her, he skidded to a stop with a wide-eyed look. Ryder glanced behind him as if debating an escape, and her stomach started hurting again. He didn't want to be here. He was here out of politeness.

His ruddy brows furrowed, he wound through the crowd until he reached her. "Hey."

Desperate to protect herself from rejection, Lexi said, "It's okay. I'm super busy, and you probably want to try a bunch of food. We'll just see each other around town sometime."

Ryder looked dumbfounded. "What?"

Lexi puffed air out of her cheeks and then busied herself with making the next batch of mini-cheesesteaks. "You don't look like you want to be here."

"I don't."

No two words had ever felt like a pair of

individual slaps before, but these did. "Then go."

"I wasn't going to come, but then I would be this asshole who didn't follow through, and you deserve better than that. Better than me."

"Oh, my gosh, okay. Enough. I get it. I really do. You can save your 'it's not you, it's me' speech. We don't even know each other."

"No, I mean, I'm gonna fuck this up," Ryder said on a rushed breath.

Lexi froze, a strip of thinly sliced steak dangling from her tongs. Words escaped her, so Ryder tumbled on. "I'm not doing this right, and Wes told me to take it easy and slow and not to get attached, but you don't seem like the type of lady a man avoids getting attached to, you know?"

"No," she said, baffled. "I'm the exact type of woman a man can avoid getting attached to. Literally everyone I've ever dated gets bored and finds their wife immediately following a break-up with me." Or sometimes during, like Ballsack Blake did.

Ryder shoved a mini-cheesesteak in his maw and around the bite said, "I eat when I'm nervous. Holy fuck, Sexy Lexi, this is good. Can I have another? I'm gonna have another." He gulped and upended the contents of another plastic sample bowl into his maw. His chiseled jaw flexed with each chew. He apparently hadn't shaved since they'd seen each other last, and fiery stubble glinted in the saturated sunlight.

No one in the history of the universe had ever looked this sexy eating cheese and meat.

He wore a white stretch T-shirt that made his blue eyes seem even brighter somehow. It was tight on his broad shoulders and slightly looser at his tapered waist. At least he'd lost the short shorts and was wearing medium-wash jeans today. The hem of his shirt had caught on the waistband of his pants and tucked in just slightly. He probably had an eight-pack or a ten-pack, or hell, maybe a twelve-pack. Did God make those?

"I like the way you're staring at my dick, but you're making the customers uncomfortable. Did you hear anything I said? Should I talk through my pener hole to keep your attention?"

The mayor and his two teenaged children were staring at Ryder with their mouths hanging open.

"Oh, my gosh, stop talking," she whispered. Mortified, she pressed her clammy palms onto her cheeks to cool the searing blush there. "Mayer Hawkins, I'm so sorry."

"Mayor Hawkins?" Ryder asked. Oh God, he was going to make this worse. But he reached over and shook the mayor's hand and introduced himself like a normal person. "I'm Ryder Croy."

Ronnie Hawkins, the mayor's sixteen-year-old son, said, "Hey, I know you! I follow you online. You're Air Ryder. *The* Air Ryder! Dad," he said, turning his grin on his father, "he's the snowy owl! He's one of the Bloodrunners."

"Aaah," Mayor Hawkins said. "It's a pleasure to meet you. I was actually wanting to welcome your crew to town." He lowered his voice. "Between you and me, you did Bryson City a big favor when you chased the vamps out of the area. Aric was all right, but his coven was in trouble all the time."

"Glad we could help," Ryder said. He winked at Ronnie, who was gawking.

"Can I have your autograph? My girlfriend isn't going to believe I talked to you if I don't bring her proof."

Ryder chuckled warmly. "Sure, kid."

Stunned, Lexi fumbled for the pen she'd been

using to tally how many samples she'd given out today and handed it to Ryder. He asked Ronnie his name and scribbled across a napkin, then signed his name like he'd done it a thousand times. Hell, maybe he had.

"Your mushrooms are burning," Ryder said helpfully.

Lexi squawked and rushed to stir them. After she emptied the pan on the big griddle next to the steak and added cheese on top to melt, she looked up to find Ryder pulling on plastic gloves.

"Bark!"

Ryder spun around with a hopeful look on his face, but he frowned suspiciously at the champagne-colored Chihuahua sitting up in her cushy bed. "What is that?"

"That's my dog, Sprinkles."

"No ma'am," he growled. "That's two pounds wet and covered in pink jewels. Sprinkles?" He offered Lexi an offended glare. "That's not a dog. It's a husky hamster."

"Grrrrr."

Lexi giggled at the tiny, unintimidating rattle in her dog's throat. "Sprinkles doesn't take shit from anyone, Ryder. Stop judging her."

"Or what? She'll lick me to death? Is that a tutu? You put a pink tutu on her?" He shook his head and started organizing the samples into neat rows. "That's not right." But he didn't look mad. In fact, a smile crept across his lips every time he looked back at Sprinkles.

Lexi got the feeling that Ryder was more of a softy than he let on.

The next hour passed in a blur as they settled into a routine together. Ryder handed out samples and chatted up the event-goers until eventually they began gathering and talking around Lexi's tent. The ebb and flow of laughter as old friends caught up around them made Lexi's heart happy. Ryder was a capable man who seemed to adapt instantly to what needed to be done, and before long, he was working with her side-by-side, bringing her supplies from the giant cooler, cooking the mushrooms and onions, cutting the steak, sectioning off the filling for the miniature hoagie rolls, the whole nine. And all while charming the socks off the people who visited her—their—tent.

No one was more charmed than Lexi, though.

Maybe it was his comfortable, friendly nature, or his ease at conversing with strangers. Perhaps it was that he could place a witty one-liner perfectly, or that he made the kids giggle and always reflected their smile as though he truly enjoyed making people happy. But it was also the way he looked people directly in their eyes as if they were the only ones in the world he wanted to talk to. It was the way one side of his lips curved up higher than the other when he laughed. It was the way his blue eyes danced, turned intense, and then danced again every time he cast her a glance—which was often. It was the way he brushed her hip with his fingertips when he needed her to move over but let his touch linger there, and the way he wrapped his arm around her shoulder when the crowd was happy and murmured, "You look pretty today," against her ear. It was the way his presence working beside her was unforced, and the way he kept leaning into her when he wanted to tell a joke.

She'd never giggled so much in a single afternoon in all her life.

Air Ryder Croy was either the smoothest man she'd ever met, or he was something really special.

"Last sample," Ryder declared.

"I want it!" Alana called from her tent. She jogged over, pulling off her plastic gloves as she approached. "I've been smelling these all day, and I'm starving. Gimme, gimme, gimme," she said as Ryder pretended he was going to eat it. Lexi chuckled at Alana's happy moaning sounds as she chewed.

Lexi had started packing everything up after cooking the last batch of samples and was already halfway done with Ryder's help. "This is the first time I've ever worked with a sous-chef," Lexi said.

Alana gulped her food down, and her dark eyes went round. "Ryder was helpful?"

Ryder shook his head and looked utterly disappointed. "You're about to get demoted, second best friend."

"Watch out, Alana," Lexi teased. "I'm coming for your spot."

"You can have it," Alana grumbled. "Last week Ryder asked me to check a lump in his balls."

Lexi gasped at Ryder. "Are you okay?"

Ryder was smirking, and Alana said, "He didn't have a lump in his balls. He was just trying to see if he could get me to touch his nuts. Aaron bled him for trying."

"Bled you?"

Proudly, Ryder pulled up the back of his shirt and showed off four long, silver claw marks that looked years healed. "I almost got out of his way, but Aaron had rage on his side."

"But you're in the same crew. You're friends...right?"

"Crews fight, especially the men. It's ingrained in them to brawl and usually fixes what ails them." Alana bullied the lid to the old cooler closed and carried it to the back of Lexi's jeep parked right behind the tent. Over her shoulder, Alana winked and said, "They're monsters, all of them."

But when Lexi looked at Ryder, he was squatted down in front of Sprinkles's bed, refilling her bowl with water from his half-empty plastic bottle. As he shuffled closer, Ryder reached out gently and scratched her dog behind the ears. He was a giant compared to her dog, but he was being so tender. Soothingly, Ryder murmured something too low for Lexi to hear.

That man was no monster at all.

FIVE

"Sooo," Lexi drawled as Ryder shoved the last of her supplies into the back of her Jeep. "Thanks for helping me out today."

He sat on the bumper and stretched his legs out. "I actually had fun."

"Yeah?" She sat next to him and watched the hustle and bustle of vendors packing up tents on Main Street. "No thoughts of Serena?" She shouldn't have asked that, she knew, but it was hard to get Ryder's ex out of her head completely. He'd been obviously working very hard to keep in contact with her.

Ryder crossed his arms over his chest and huffed a laugh. "You jealous?"

"No."

"Liar. How many times did you stare at my sexy picture?"

Oh! Heat flooded her cheeks for the tenth time in an hour so she looked anywhere but at him. "In my defense, it was a really interesting picture."

"It was the abs right? Or my perfect nipples?" He looked down at his chest where indeed they were puckered up against the thin material. "I was blessed with perfect nipple symmetry."

She hid her smile and leaned back against the Jeep. "I couldn't see your abs very well because of the angle, but I could definitely make out the head of your dick peeking out of those tiny shorts."

"You're welcome."

She snorted and rubbed her eyes.

"Tired?"

"I got up at four this morning to prep for the event. I'm whooped."

Ryder rested his elbows on his knees and ran his hands over the back of his head. "Can I ask you a question?" he asked without looking up.

"Is it another weird one?"

"When you told me not to call Serena back…"

Oh, this was serious. "Yeah?"

"Why?"

The soft murmurs of the packing vendors bounced this way and that, and the evening shadows stretched across Main Street. The night air chilled her skin, and she rubbed her arms to bring warmth back into them. "I guess because I heard the way she spoke to you, and I hated it. I wanted you to show her. I imagined her sitting at her computer with an evil smile, waiting for you to come crawling back, and I wanted you to be stronger than that. Stronger than her. Or maybe that's what I wish I would've done."

"What do you mean?"

"I dated someone who pulled all the strings, and I let him for a long time. I was convinced he was it for me. If I just overlooked this and overlooked that, I was compromising like I was supposed to. I was being a good girlfriend, and he would appreciate it."

"And did he?"

"No. He worked out of town, so I only saw him on the weekends, and apparently he met someone out on a job." She shrugged her shoulders up to her ears to try and stifle the shame Blake still made her feel. "He broke it off with me because he'd proposed to her."

Ryder shook his head and watched Sprinkles zooming around in front of them in her little cart with wheels.

"Blake knew he wanted to be with her for the rest of his life after cheating with her for three months. We'd been together for four years, and I hadn't managed to lock him down. I'd put in the work, put up with more than I should've, lost myself along the way, and he picked someone else behind my back. I guess when I saw Serena talking to you like that, it reminded me of how Blake used to treat me and how I'd settled for this awful existence because I'd convinced myself it was better than being alone." She nudged Ryder's shoulder with her own. "But it's not."

Sprinkles tried to climb up on the curb and got stuck, and before Lexi could move, Ryder got up and righted her in the grass, then sauntered back. And this time, when he sat on the bumper beside her, he held her hand with shocking familiarity.

Lexi stared down at their arms. Her skin was tanned from her time in the sun, and his was fair and covered with freckles. His hand was massive compared to hers, and calloused, but so warm, so strong. Steady.

He dragged a troubled gaze to hers and murmured, "Blake's an asshole, so is Serena, and tonight we both move on. You don't have to ask me about her anymore."

"What about Dottie?"

Ryder scratched his red facial scruff with the back of his thumbnail and sighed. "She ain't mine to worry about anymore. I gave her to Serena when she was a puppy. Little mangy mutt I found at the shelter, but I thought maybe Dottie would open up Serena's maternal instincts. She was terrible with kids, and I wanted them somethin' fierce. But Serena didn't open up. She looked at Dottie as a burden, so she became my baby, you know? I was gonna hire a lawyer to fight for the dog, but because I gave her as a gift, my chances were slim to none at keeping her. Serena emptied our joint account, bought herself a sixty-thousand-dollar SUV right before we broke up, and since we shared the damn account, she got away with it. I didn't have any money to spend on a lawyer that probably wouldn't get me my dog back."

"Oh Ryder, I'm so sorry. So her talking about you

not having a job?"

"Is bullshit. I grew up as a logger by trade with the crew I was born into. Moved away from the Boarlanders and went to welding school and made good money at it. I hated the hours, though. It was two weeks on, one off on a rig, and I was miserable, but Serena liked the income. So yeah, when I would come home, and she was bitching at me for this and that, I would go off with my buddies and drink just to get a few minutes where I felt normal. Where I could feel like not everyone hated me. The worst part," he said, squeezing her hand. "The absolute worst was when I came here for the first time. Wyatt was in deep with vamps and wolves, fighting to buy some land to try and help Harper out."

"Your alpha?"

"Yeah, but at the time she was just one of my good friends. She was real sick, and her days were numbered unless her dragon could choose a treasure. Wyatt was trying to do that for her, give her the mountains. He needed money, and I could've helped if he'd come to me a few months before that, before Serena emptied me out. I think that was my breaking point when I didn't want to consider chasing her anymore. I was in it for Dottie after that."

"How long were you with Serena?"

"Three years."

"Why didn't you propose?"

He gave a single, dark laugh. "I did. She wouldn't have me. Not like that. I did what you did, waited around for her to be ready, but I wasn't it for her, you know? I wasn't the one."

"We make quite the pathetic pair," Lexi murmured.

"Ha!" Ryder's laugh echoed down the street as he draped his arm over her shoulders, still clasping her hand in his. "Speak for yourself. I'm awesome."

Lexi giggled and shook her head for the tenth time today. She liked his sense of humor more than she wanted to admit out loud.

"How did a professional chef land in small-town North Carolina?" Ryder asked.

"Well the small-town part wasn't in my plans. I went to school around here, grew up with Alana, actually. And I couldn't wait to get out of here after graduation. I thought the people who were staying here after high school were settling, you know? Like they would never see the world and always be small town."

"Snooty snooty."

"So snooty," she said with a chuckle. "I went to culinary school in Chicago and landed a job right after I graduated, aaaand," she drawled out.

"You hated it."

"I hated it," she agreed. "I missed small-town living and knowing everyone. I missed people asking about my day and waving to me when I drove by them on the street. I just got to this point where I felt like a number, and I couldn't fix this void in my chest. And for some reason, every time I came back to visit for the holidays, I felt a million times better. It was like a soul-recharge every time I came back, and eventually, I just didn't want to go back to my job at the fancy restaurant in a town I hadn't connected to and feel empty anymore." Lexi shrugged. "So I stayed."

"And the void is gone now?" Ryder asked in a careful voice.

"It is. I feel like I belong here. Hell, maybe I always did belong, and I just needed to leave to see how good I had it. This place is home, and I love my job. I get to use my culinary skills in a small cabin setting where I actually get to talk to the clients I cook for. I like this much more than being in a hot kitchen ten hours a day getting verbally maimed by the head chef every two minutes. I get to set up my own clients and build rapport. I'm happier here than I was in Chicago. I don't know. Maybe that means the big city defeated me."

"Nah, you just figured out what you want. There's no defeat in that."

Sprinkles tried to get off the curb but got stuck. She looked right at Ryder for help.

Lexi made an offended sound in her throat. "Traitor."

Ryder bit Lexi's knuckles gently, then released her and jogged over to help Sprinkles. "You would've had a shot at fealty if your dog was a boy, but the ladies love me."

Lexi frowned as she watched the giant, sexy, musclebound man right Sprinkles's little wheels onto the concrete. And Lexi could see it. From the hundreds of thousands of followers online and the flirty comments girls put all over his posts, to the way he'd charmed the masses today with little effort, Ryder had no reason to settle with a single woman.

He'd grown a massive following not only for the way he looked, and the animal he wielded, but also by the force of his personality.

Everyone knew his name—Air Ryder.

He could have whoever he wanted.

"What's that look for?" Ryder asked, locking his arms on either side of her hips. He leaned in so close her breath froze in her chest.

Slowly, he lifted a finger and brushed it against her eyebrow, smoothing her frown away.

She'd done her research about shifters, and even flight shifters could hear a lie, so she didn't even try. "You scare me."

Ryder eased back by inches, studied her face. "I'm in control of my animal. I would never hurt you."

"That's not what I mean."

His face went slack with realization. For a moment, he was right there, locked in her gaze, and she witnessed the change in his eyes firsthand. They morphed from blue to a bright gold that was almost hard to look at...almost. He dipped his gaze to her lips, and this was it. He was going to kiss her, and it would make him even more terrifying. She would fall in love without him, because that's what she did. She picked men who were unavailable.

"Ryder," she said on a breath. At some point, she had to learn her lesson and protect herself.

"I'm not what you think I am," he whispered. Slowly, he leaned forward and pressed his lips to hers.

She'd imagined this moment in the build-up to today. Imagined what his lips would feel like on hers, but she'd come nowhere close to the real thing. The rasp of his beard prickled against her soft face, such a contrast. Rough man, soft woman. But his lips were easy against hers, forming perfectly to match hers. He angled his head and sipped at her, and she could feel it. The slight brush of his tongue on her closed lips.

This was the moment when she should ease away and tell him she wasn't ready, but she couldn't put space between them, no matter how hard she tried. There was this pull, like she was metal and he was a magnet. Fighting the attraction would do no good.

Weak.

No, some inner voice said. *Not weak. Happy.*

He did make her happy.

Parting her lips slightly, she allowed him in on

the next pass, his tongue dipping into her mouth. He tasted divine, and she let off a soft noise deep in her throat. She rested her palm on his cheek to feel his jaw move as he kissed her and, holy moly, no kiss had ever felt like this. It wasn't passionate lust or neediness that drove his tongue against hers, stroke after reverent stroke. He was building a slow fire in her middle so that she would burn longer and brighter.

He pulled her hand from his cheek, slowly drew it behind his neck, and stood, bringing her with him. His body was rock hard against hers, and his erection was stony between their hips, but he didn't push for more. Ryder seemed content to just tether her to him completely with this kiss.

"Do you want cheese on your burgers?" someone shouted from across the street. Whoever it was probably wasn't talking to her and Ryder.

Lexi slid her other arm around his neck and sighed a happy sound at his slow dips into her mouth.

A shrill whistle echoed. "Ryder, take a break from sucking face long enough to tell me cheese or no cheese, man. I'm about to burn this meat!"

Ryder growled and ended the kiss with a soft

smack, then yelled behind him, "Fucking surprise me, man! I'm busy!"

Lexi giggled and hid her face against Ryder's chest.

"Sooo," Aaron called. "Yes to cheese on both? Lexi? Cheese?"

"Oh, for fuck's sake," Ryder muttered. With an irritated sigh, he cocked his head and asked her, "Lexi, would you like to eat with my crew?"

"I would love to, but maybe we should wait until that goes down?" She snickered and pointed to his massive boner.

"No," Ryder said with a baffled head shake. "Come on, Sprinkles," he muttered, pulling Lexi behind him. "Interrupting Aaron can deal with an eyeful of my happy wienice, and fuck him if he mentions it."

Oh, dear goodness, he said *wienice*! Ryder seemed mad so she stifled her laughter. Lexi should be embarrassed, really she should, but Ryder had very little shame about bodily functions, so okay. She probably smelled like a vat of pheromones, and the shifters had heightened senses, but they would also have to get over that because Ryder was right.

Interrupting Aaron would just have to deal with the consequences of his actions.

"Beer," Aaron said, handing Lexi and Ryder a pair of cold cans as they approached.

"Are we allowed to be drinking out here?" Lexi asked, scanning the still blocked off street for Officer Darby. He was a stickler about public consumption of alcohol.

"Drink it fast if you're worried about getting caught," a chestnut-haired man with bright blue eyes said. He held out a hand for a shake. "I'm Wyatt."

"Lexi," she said with a grin.

"That's my mate Harper over there beside Alana."

Wyatt gestured to a brunette with oddly colored eyes, one brown and one blue with a long pupil like Kane's. There was the dragon-blooded alpha. A wave of fear washed through Lexi as she waved politely, but that eased the second Harper pulled an old bag chair closer to hers and patted the seat. "We saved you a spot."

Okay then. Lexi moved to sit down, but Ryder pulled her back gently and hugged her close, lowered his lips to her ear and murmured, "I know you're tired, but thank you for saying yes to hanging out with my people."

She sighed out a shaky breath and clutched his shirt when she swayed slightly on her feet. His deep voice against her ear had her insides tingling.

"I'll take care of everything," Ryder promised. "Just relax tonight, okay?"

Unable to form a single word due to the wrecking ball he'd just sent sailing through her ovaries, she nodded dumbly and then squeaked in shock when he grabbed her ass hard and bit her neck with a chomping sound. "Sexy little Lexi," he growled, and when she looked back up at him, his eyes were the color of the sun. Air Ryder was the sexy one.

She stumbled this way and that over to the chair and almost dropped her beer as she sank into the fabric seat. Sprinkles was running circles in the middle of everyone, tongue hanging out as she panted happily through her doggy smile. Sprinkles looked like Lexi felt.

"You okay?" Harper asked, her delicate, dark eyebrows arched high and a knowing grin on her lips.

Lexi inhaled deeply, and on the exhale said, "I think that man is gonna wreck me."

Although the thought had frightened her when they'd been sitting on the bumper of her Jeep, now, as Ryder watched her with that inhuman, hungry gaze of his, Lexi suddenly felt like that prospect had never been more exciting.

****

True to his word, Ryder had taken care of her completely. He'd brought her food and a second beer. He'd pulled up a chair next to hers and settled her legs in his lap as if they'd been lovers for years. She adored this easy and instant comfort with another person, but a part of her was scared Ryder was this familiar with every woman he met. What if she wasn't special to him? She'd watched him lock gazes with person after person today and convince them they were the person he wanted to talk to most in the world.

He was a charmer, so why was she losing her heart so hard to him right now? Had she learned nothing from Blake?

But then Ryder would lift her knuckles to his lips right in the middle of saying something to his crew, kiss her, and rest her palm back on his thigh, as though he didn't even notice he was doing it. That meant something, right? It sure meant a helluva lot to her. And then he'd gone and unstrapped Sprinkles from her cart when she'd worn down, lifted her against his chest, and with little effort at all, put her to sleep like a teeny baby.

And now Lexi's lady bits pulsed once at the sight of Ryder stroking Sprinkles little body with his thumb while he rested his other hand on Lexi's and rubbed gentle little circles on her knuckles.

Was this really happening right now?

Sprinkles snored loudly. Nope, definitely not a dream.

"Kane!" Wyatt called, his hands cupped around his mouth.

The black-haired man climbing into an old Bronco across the street paused and looked their way.

Wyatt waved him over.

"He won't do it," murmured Wes.

"Five bucks says he will," Ryder said.

"You're on," the Novak Raven said.

"I think I'm gonna call it a night," Kane called out.

"Told you," Wes said with a sneer.

"I bet Wes five bucks you would hang out!"

Ryder yelled. "Don't let my faith in you go to waste."

"Cheater," Wes muttered.

Lexi was human, but even she could hear Kane's gritted out "mother fucker" from here. He looked pissed as he crossed the street. He flipped his dark hair, longer on top, to the other side in an irritated gesture. Dark sunglasses covered his face as usual. He liked to hide his dragon eyes from the town, but Lexi had seen them once at Drat's Boozehouse when he was arm wrestling one of the locals.

"Pay up, suckaaah," Ryder crowed at Weston. Sprinkles twitched in the cradle of his arm but didn't wake.

Kane looked uncomfortable as hell as he looked around at all the full seats, but he needn't worry. "Take mine," Lexi offered.

Ryder was already pulling her into his lap anyway, the snuggler. But as his erection poked her butt cheek, she thought maybe it wasn't so much snuggling on his mind as other intimacies. His waggling red eyebrows backed that theory.

She laughed and relaxed against him as the chatter of the crew picked up again. Kane was quiet like he always was, but after a few minutes, Lexi spied his first smile. How many times had she seen him around town, or at the bar when she'd gone to cut loose after bad days at work? A dozen? Fifteen? She'd maybe seen him smile a handful of times, but tonight, the longer he spent with the crew, the more his lips curved up.

"Lexi, you'll like this one. We used to call him Karate Ryder," Wyatt said with a laugh as he pointed the neck of his beer bottle at Ryder.

"Because I was awesome at karate," Ryder said confidently.

"No, you were terrible," Wes said. He arched his eyebrows at Lexi. "From age twelve to fourteen, he was the most annoying kid you could ever meet. Every sleepover, Karate Kid movies. Every day after school, karate moves in the woods. Every dinner conversation—"

"Let me guess, karate?" Lexi asked.

"Exactly. And he sucked at it."

"False," Ryder said. "I surpassed my master in under a year."

Harper snorted. "You got kicked out of class because you refused to take direction."

With a chuckle, Ryder argued, "That's because I

knew everything."

He was trying to hide a smile again, and Lexi rolled her eyes.

The others launched into a discussion about how a Boarlander bear shifter named Bash used to make them pizza rolls after school and tutor them in math. Ryder had gone quiet, though, and pulled the hairband gently out of Lexi's ponytail, loosing her long hair. His fingers were firm as he massaged the back of her neck. He watched her face with a slight frown. "You feel different."

"What do you mean?" she murmured, relaxing into his massage.

He was quiet for a minute before he answered, "Forget it. I don't know what I mean."

Well, that was a copout if she'd ever heard one. He ran his fingertips up the back of her head, through her hair, and massaged until she curled her legs in his lap around Sprinkles and sighed happily.

The early spring wind kicked up, and even though Ryder was warm as a furnace against her, she'd only worn a T-shirt with her job logo on it, and gooseflesh rose across her arms.

"You cold?"

"A little." Oh, he made her so mushy with how much he cared.

"Sad, little human with your pathetically thin skin," Ryder said with a shake of his head.

Lexi swatted his chest. "I'm super tough, I'll have you know."

"Oh, I can tell from your shivering. Crew, I'm gonna see this one off." Ryder rocked them up out of the chair and settled her on her feet.

"Neeeew," Alana drawled. "It's still early."

"Ha, early for you party animals," Lexi teased. "Get it?"

"Party. *Animals*," Ryder said, finishing her joke with a snicker.

Wes, Aaron, and Wyatt shook their heads in mock disappointment.

"But really," Lexi said. "I have to make breakfast for a couple up at the cabins in the morning, and that five a.m. alarm comes quick."

"You said comes quick," Ryder repeated through a smirk.

She giggled and leaned over to pat Kane on the leg as she passed. Quick as a strike of lightning, he grabbed her hand just before she touched his knee.

His face had gone stone hard, and his grip was too tight.

"If you want to keep those fuckin' dragon eyes in your face, I suggest you let her go," Ryder said blandly.

Kane relaxed his grip and murmured a hasty apology. Then without another word, he stood and limped past Harper and Wyatt's chairs and across the street to his ride.

Lexi watched him blast out of his parking space as she rubbed her sore hand gingerly. "Is that a rule? No touching?" she asked. "I didn't mean to chase him off."

"Nah," Ryder said. "That's just Kane's rules. Most shifters thrive on affection, especially from their crew and mates. Kane never had a crew, though. He didn't learn." Ryder had said it lightly, but when Lexi looked up at him, a slight frown marred his striking red eyebrows, and he was staring at Kane's taillights.

Her distress evaporated when she saw Sprinkles. Ryder had her on her back, cradled to his chest like a little baby, and she was looking up at him adoringly, her back legs limp against his arm. How fucking cute to see a strapping, musclebound, filthy-mouthed behemoth carrying her little hairy baby so gently.

Lexi picked up Sprinkles's cart and made to leave. Harper and Alana hugged her farewell, and as she passed, Wes grabbed her hand suddenly. He held her there, locking her in his gaze as his bright green eyes tightened at the corners. And after the span of a couple of heartbeats, he released her grip and relaxed back into his chair. "Nothing," he murmured in a satisfied tone.

"What was that about?" Lexi murmured as she and Ryder walked toward her Wrangler.

"Wes has some kind of fucked-up future teller sight. I guess he thought if he molested your hand, he would see something about you."

"Wait, he can see the future?"

"He could before Alana was Turned. He had visions bad, but he hasn't had any in the last few months. I guess that was the test. I guess he can't see you."

Ryder's tone had darkened on that last part, so she studied his face in the illumination of the street lights that lined the road. He was suddenly very busy looking at Sprinkles.

"I feel like you only like me for my dog," she

teased.

"Not true. I fell for your tits first."

Her surprised laugh echoed down the street, and before she could change her mind, Lexi wrapped her arms around his waist and fell into step beside him. After a moment of hesitation, he draped his empty arm around her shoulders and pulled her tightly against his side, pressed his lips against her hairline.

She felt like she was glowing under his affection. If she could see herself in this moment, there would be a soft, happy aura clinging to her like a second skin. She was falling hard for Ryder, and it left her a bit breathless.

"Do all owl shifters like affection?" she asked softly as they reached her jacked-up Jeep.

"Uuuh, I'm not sure. There aren't many snowy owls."

"How many are there?" she asked curiously, resting her back against the door as Ryder settled Sprinkles in the back.

"Me and my mom that I know of. There has to be more, but they're in hiding or maybe dead. None but me and my mom have registered."

"Oh." That sounded lonely.

"Well, don't pity me, woman. I have my mom, and my dad is a shifter, too."

"What kind?"

"A boar."

"Wait, *the* boar shifter?" There was only one registered as far as she knew, and the only reason she remembered was because he had a very specific, very intimidating name. "Your dad is the Beast Boar?"

"Yep. He took me in as his own when my real dad bailed. And I was brought up in a good crew. Well, my crew was bat-shit crazy, but they were family. I had good role models. But yeah." He leaned his back on her Jeep beside her. "I think owl shifters are affectionate. I grew up watching my mom just *melt* against my dad when she saw him after a long day. They would stand in the kitchen for half an hour, not saying anything, just hugging each other." Ryder swallowed hard. "I want that—being able to make someone's day better just by holding them."

"You're a romantic."

"No, I'm not. I'm very manly and unromantic. Cock, dick, finger-bang, tit-suck—"

"Okay." She bit her lip against a smile. Ryder could deny it all he wanted, but he was straight from one of the romantic movies she liked to watch—but with a filthy mouth, a dirty mind, and a chronic boner.

"So, as far as first friend-dates go…"

"Yeah?" she asked.

"How would you rate this one?"

Lexi puffed air out her cheeks and felt like she was floating. He cared what she thought of today. "Ten out of ten for me. You?" she asked, trying to hide the hope from her voice.

Ryder gave her a sideways glance, and that sexy smile that took the corner of his lips was back. "Same."

Gently, he pulled her in front of him between his splayed legs and dragged her hips close.

Lexi ran her hands up his muscular chest and settled her palms just under his collar bones. "How are you so warm?" she whispered in awe.

"Snowy owl," he murmured. "I'm made for the cold."

"I'm always cold. It's hard for me to get warm."

He angled his head, his eyes turning a muddier color, from blue to light brown. "We fit."

She rested her forehead against his chest and

shook her head in disbelief that just a couple of words from his lips could affect her heartrate like this. Her chest was pounding like a drum, and as she stilled against him, his was doing the same thing, as if their hearts were racing each other. Oh, she was in trouble with this one.

"Bark!"

Lexi checked on her dog around Ryder's wide shoulders, and the little Chihuahua had pulled her body right next to the door and was looking up at them with her tongue lolled out.

"Jealous," Lexi accused. "He's mine right now."

The grin slipped from Ryder's face in an instant. "Say that again," he murmured.

"She's jealous."

"No, the other part."

Lexi hesitated until she knew her voice would come out steady. Then she ran her hands down his chest and linked their hands. "You're mine right now."

Ryder looked down the street and blew out a long breath. "Woman, you're making this real hard to take our friendship slow."

"I don't know what you mean," she said

innocently.

"No, you know exactly what you're doin'." He gripped her waist tighter in his big, strong hands. "Everything in me wants to drive you to a back road, pull over, and flip you over in that backseat."

"And do what?" she asked on a shocked breath.

"You know what."

And oh, she could see it—her ass in the air, tits brushing the seat fabric, getting pounded from behind by Ryder, his powerful body flexing against hers as he drove her to release. The warmth in her middle turned to magma, and her breath trembled on every exhale.

Ryder lifted his chin but kept his now-gold eyes on hers. "You smell sexy as fuck, Lexi." He pulled her harder against his long, thick erection and murmured, "I'm about to start making real bad decisions if I don't say goodnight to you now."

Did she want that? Did she want to say goodnight and get her head back on straight, or did she want to give two flying middle fingers to caution and get herself taken by the Air Ryder?

"Woman, stop lookin' at me like you want my dick buried inside of you, or it'll happen. I'm trying to do this right."

She opened her mouth to tell him she definitely wanted to be bad and do dirty things with him, but Sprinkles barked again. And at that interruption, Ryder was now looking mighty determined to slow them down. Sprinkles was a cock blocker.

Ryder eased her back and opened her door, then waited there, arms locked against the opening as she buckled in.

She didn't want to leave him. Tonight had been amazing. The whole day had been. She'd settled into something so comfortable and interesting with him in just a few meetings, and today had sealed her heart to him. But she couldn't be that girl—the one who begged for more time when he was clearly saying goodbye. She'd done that before and had more pride now. She could tell him something else, though, something she felt compelled to share.

"Ryder?" she asked quickly before he could shut her door.

"Yeah?"

She used his words from earlier because she felt them down to her marrow. "You feel different to me, too."

Ryder's gold eyes sparked with intensity as he leaned into the front of her jeep. He cupped her neck and pressed his lips to hers. He wasn't patient like with their first kiss. This time, he plunged his tongue past her lips, demanding she let him in, demanding to taste her.

She slid her hands over his shoulders and gripped the back of his hair, raking her nails against his scalp. Ryder's reaction was instant, pressing her against the seat, kissing her so hard it stole the breath from her lungs. God, she loved this. Loved the way he tasted, loved the way his lips were moved on hers, loved the way his mouth fit hers so perfectly. She'd never met a man who could kiss her like this. One who could make her forget where she was. Ryder had the uncanny ability to make the rest of the world fade away to nothing.

He pulled her hand from around his neck and pressed her palm against his chest, right over his pounding heartbeat. She smiled against his lips. How could someone make her feel this happy? This okay? This whole? This wanted?

Perhaps Weston had visions of the future, but Air Ryder was magic.

He bit her bottom lip gently and disengaged, gave her a peck, and then another and another, each getting more gentle until he eased away completely.

Without a word, he tugged her cell phone from the cup holder, saved his number into it, then called his phone. She was glad he was handling the number-swap because right now her arms and legs were numb and her fingers probably wouldn't work on account of him kissing her so thoroughly.

He pulled her hand to his lips, kissed her knuckles, then backed out of the car and shut the door. Right. Now she had to remember how to drive.

And just like he had on the side of the road, Ryder watched her leave. Except this time when Lexi glanced in her rearview mirror, he didn't look troubled.

He looked hopeful instead.

SIX

Ryder dropped the stack of logs from their resting spot on his shoulder to the ground. They clattered and scattered, but without a single second's break, he strode back into the woods to grab the others he'd felled.

He and Wes had dreamed of starting a business like this since they were kids, but then they'd grown up, moved out of Damon's Mountains, and lived in different places. Ryder had become a welder and Wes a logger, and he'd never thought this would be possible—their childhood dream.

But then Harper had called them in to give Wyatt some backup, and the small reunion with old friends had turned into so much more. They'd all landed an unexpected crew, and yeah, sometimes it was hell trying to figure everything out with the Bloodrunners, but this right here—the opportunity to follow through on a dream with his best friend—made Ryder feel like maybe he was supposed to end up here with the Bloodrunners all along.

Then he'd met Lexi. And holy shit, he'd never encountered a more terrifying woman. She had grown the ability, in an overwhelmingly short amount of time, to destroy him completely. Serena had tried and failed to break him, along with the other women he'd tried to bond with, but Lexi had power she didn't realize yet.

Maybe he should keep it hidden from her. Maybe he should slow them down, or even grind them to a halt until he could wrap his head around how much he liked her. Wes had told him to take it slow, and the fact remained that not only had the Gray Back Crew's seer, Beaston, not seen Ryder with a mate, but Wes hadn't seen it either. That bothered Ryder.

When Alana had come along for Aaron, Weston had been pummeled with visions of her with shifter eyes. He'd known she would be Turned, known she would be a Bloodrunner without a shadow of a doubt.

But he saw nothing of Lexi?

Not only that, but he was acting strange. Ryder knew Wes better than anyone, and he'd never given two shits about bonds, relationships, or claiming a mate. But since Ryder had mentioned Lexi, he was cool-as-you-like about him dating her. And Ryder couldn't help but think it was because Wes didn't take their relationship seriously. It felt like Wes didn't care if he dated Lexi or not because he didn't believe she would be in his life long-term.

Was he reading into Weston's behavior too deeply? Maybe. But nothing else he'd come up with explained why his best friend wasn't fighting Ryder's interest in Lexi.

And Ryder so badly wanted her to be more than just another woman passing through his life.

She felt special. When he hugged her, touched her, kissed her, or even looked at her, there was this bright spot in his middle that seemed to pulse with devotion.

A week since he'd first met her, and Ryder had been prepared to call out Kane's motherfuckin' Blackwing Dragon to brawl for grabbing Lexi's hand too hard.

He was doing it again.

He was making the same mistake he made every time a woman showed interest. He locked onto her, suffocated her until she acted out and ultimately rejected him. And he was so fucking tired of rejection.

He'd been shouldering that since he was a baby. *No, don't think about him.* Robbie Anderson was a prick and a leaver. Dwelling on him wouldn't do anything but put Ryder in a tail-spin, and he was over that. He'd gone through his angry phase as a teenager. Ryder allowing his biological dad to affect his life took away from all that Mason did for him. God, he wished he could just cut all memories of his real dad from his head and start on the day he'd met Mason. Why the fuck were his memories at age four and five so vivid? They should've faded, but they were there in the back of his mind, the brightest memories that made up the darkest parts of him.

Fuck Robbie.

Ryder should've been born to Mason. He should have Beast Boar blood pumping through his veins.

Absently, Ryder ran his finger over the old scar Mason had cut just under his collar bone. That's what the boars did to declare someone was theirs, and when Ryder had asked, Mason had cut him immediately. Mason had never rejected him, so why the hell was Ryder stuck in this unending hiccup over his biological father leaving him?

Because he left you.

It wasn't like Robbie and Mom split up and his real dad had just drifted away. No, Robbie had tried to keep a relationship with Ryder, but Robbie had hated him so much, he couldn't stand to be a part of his life. He'd said it over and over. *Sometimes I really hate you, you little freak.*

And then he'd signed his parental rights over just so he wouldn't have to see Ryder again.

Freak.

"Fuck," Ryder choked out as he gripped his hair.

Riding this loop wasn't doing any good. It would only hurt worse the deeper he dug into the whys and what ifs.

He had to dig out of the past if he wanted a shot at making a woman like Lexi happy. He couldn't go through his whole life dragging the ghost of his dad. It would haunt him, haunt Lexi, haunt everything he tried to accomplish, and Robbie didn't deserve that kind of power.

He never had.

****

Okay, there was the next marker. A red ribbon was tied around a tree trunk ahead. Lexi drove a washed-out road with two divots that tires had etched into the earth to create a single lane. Knee-high weeds comprised the center strip, and the brush and brambles *ping-pinged* against the undercarriage of Lexi's Jeep.

The dirt track had seemed to go on forever since she'd turned off the main road, but Alana had assured her this would lead to Ryder.

Geez, she hoped he liked surprises. What if he was out here with another woman? *Stop it. Ryder isn't Blake.* But she and Ryder hadn't called each other anything more than friends. If he was dating other women, she would have to understand.

She rocked through a deep mud hole and passed the red ribbon, then curved around with the road. There was a clearing ahead with a foundation and framework up for a building. Beside the structure, Ryder was squatted down in the grass with his hands behind his head, his shoulders heaving. "Oh, my gosh," she murmured, pulling to a stop. She shoved open the door and bolted for him, but by the time she was halfway there, Ryder stood and offered her a smile. Only it wasn't a real smile. It was too tight and didn't reach his bright gold eyes.

"Are you hurt?"

Ryder huffed, and the frail smile left his lips as he stared off into the woods. "What are you doing here?"

She cast her getaway vehicle a quick glance. "This was a bad idea. I shouldn't have just come out here like this. I'm sorry. Uuum, if you want to grab coffee or something later this week, just give me a call."

She turned and made her way toward her jeep, but something blurred past her and then Ryder's hands were on her shoulders, forcing her to a stop. "I'm sorry. You just...caught me at a bad time. I didn't want you to see..." Ryder inhaled a big breath and shook his head. "I'm sorry," he repeated.

She couldn't meet his eyes right now because the color was so light and so bright. Clutching the hem of his white T-shirt, she murmured, "Are you okay?"

"Hell yeah, I'm okay. My girl came to visit me. You want the tour?" His voice was upbeat now as if the last minute hadn't happened.

She didn't like being shut out, but he seemed determined. Ryder grabbed her hand and tugged her toward the framework building.

"I'm rebuilding my job, my life, myself right now, and this is where it started." Ryder pulled her in front of him and rested his hands on top of her shoulders. "Wes and I are starting up a business called Big Flight ATV Tours."

"Really?" she asked, floored.

"Yeah. We have twelve ATVs we are fixing up for clients. This will be the office where the tours are booked, and we are leasing the land behind this property to build trails. We'll do a beginner trail and an intermediate one. We've already scoped out the best places for scenic views of the Smokies and photo-ops. We have the company incorporated already and everything. Once we finish building the office, we'll be able to immediately start booking tours."

"Ryder," she breathed, scanning the lush green woods. "This is going to be incredible! With all the tourism around here, an ATV excursion is such a good start-up. I can make up flyers for you and give them to the concierge at Smoky Mountain Paradise

Cabins. Our clients will eat this up!" Excitement zinged through her as she looked at the building again. She could just imagine it. Rustic office, rocking chairs on the porch for the clients waiting for tours, snacks and waters inside, maybe a little shop with T-shirts and promotional water bottles and keychains.

"Come here," Ryder said excitedly, dragging her behind him around the side of the building. "The bathrooms will be here, and the gear room will be here where we fit clients with helmets and the right protective clothes if they don't come prepared. Back there in the shade, we'll have a few picnic tables. Wes is building those right now. We still have some woods to clear and to get some gravel on the road." He flicked his fingertips to the road she'd come in on. "A welcome sign still needs to be built over there, but look." He gestured to a massive garage in the woods. The doors were open, and there were rows of quads sitting ready in there.

"And you won't have to work those crazy welding shifts anymore!"

Ryder rounded on her and cupped her cheeks, his eyes feverish with excitement. "Yes," he whispered. "I *knew* you would get it. I knew you wouldn't think this was silly."

"How could I think this is silly? Ryder!" she looked around at what he and Wes were creating. "I have a really, really good feeling about this."

His smile was genuine again, stunning. White, straight teeth and dancing eyes that were morphing back to a happy blue color. He'd shaved today, so she could see his dimples and smile lines clearly.

"You want to go for a ride? I want to show you something."

She gripped his wrists to keep his hands on her cheeks and beamed up at him. "Yes! But can we bring the picnic I brought? I haven't eaten since breakfast."

His face went serious, and he dropped his voice an octave. "You brought food?"

She giggled and nodded. "I wanted to surprise you."

"You're tryin' to get yourself boned, aren't you?"

"Stop," she said, shoving off him.

In a rush, Ryder hefted her over his shoulder so fast her breathless laugh got caught in her throat. He pulled the hem of her tank top up and bit her side.

"Ow!" she howled, smacking him hard on the butt. She wished she could stop giggling, but she loved this. She adored how playful Ryder was and was so relieved he wasn't sad anymore.

"Did you bring my baby?"

"*My* baby, and no. I left Sprinkles resting at home. I want you all to myself tonight."

"What color are your panties?" Ryder pulled the waist of her jean shorts to the side.

Lexi swatted at his hand. "None of your business."

"Purple with pink polka dots? I fuckin' love that. Does your bra match?"

"Wouldn't you like to know?"

"Yes. Yes, I would." He set her on her feet by her Jeep and hooked one finger into the low scoop neck of her tank top. He arched his red eyebrows high, daring her to stop him from pulling it down.

With a put-upon sigh, Lexi pulled down the neck of her tank top until it rested under her bra, which did, in fact, match her panties.

"Sheeeyit, woman," Ryder said, standing back to admire. "That's the best set of tits I've ever laid eyes on."

He reached for her, hands cupped and ready, but she danced away from him and pulled her tank top back into place. "Feed me before you fondle me."

Ryder squared up to her, hands on her hips and head ducked down. He lowered his voice. "I want to high five your pelvis with my pelvis."

"Ryder," she warned, trying hard for a straight face.

"I want to touch belly buttons."

"Stop." Now she had to bite her lip hard not to laugh.

Ryder lowered his voice to a seductive whisper. "Let's make our nipples kiss."

Lexi peeled into giggles and hugged him up tight. Ryder lifted her off the ground and squeezed her ribs. She could feel his smile against her cheek as his warm chuckle reverberated right next to her ear.

"I missed you big time, perv," she told him.

Ryder leaned in and sucked her neck hard until she peeled into another fit of giggles. "I missed you, too."

"Oh yeah?"

"Hell yeah, trouble. I pumped the python, like, a dozen times since I saw you last."

"Oh, my gosh, did you just call your dick a python? And wait, a dozen times? You're lying. You just saw me two days ago!"

"Yep, probably gonna do it another dozen times tonight after that little tit-tease you gave me. I'm just gonna be blowin' dust."

Lexi couldn't breathe. She was doubled over laughing like a braying donkey, holding her middle because her abs were hurting so bad.

Ryder pulled her up and kissed her unexpectedly. His kiss was rough, and her giggles turned to chuckles, then to soft needy sounds as he worked her mouth. He eased her back against the Jeep and deepened their kiss, brushed his tongue against hers over and over until her legs buckled. He backed his mouth off hers with a soft, sexy smack, then rested his forehead against hers. "I wanted to taste you while you were laughing."

"And?" she asked.

"Fucking perfect." He pushed his hands off the Jeep and left her weak-kneed and wanting, the tease. Chuckling like he found himself very amusing, Ryder pulled the cooler and rolled-up, red blanket out of the back seat. "What did you bring me?"

"I cooked the last meal of a couple's vacation at lunch, and they had no need for the leftovers since they're headed to the airport tonight. I don't know where you live, so I called Alana and asked where you were so I could surprise you."

"Best surprise ever. Unless you showed up bare-ass naked. Then that would be the best surprise ever." Ryder winked and made a *tick* sound behind his teeth. "Tip for next time. Oh, my God, is this blackened catfish and alexander sauce?" he asked as he stared down into a plastic container.

"Yep! It's got some kick, too."

"Woman, you're gonna get an owl baby put in you today."

Lexi laughed, but really, that didn't scare her as much as it probably should. Ryder was going to make a very good daddy for some lucky kid someday. She could tell with how tender he was with Sprinkles and how he'd genuinely loved engaging with children the other day at the Taste of Bryson City.

Ryder led her down a squishy trail toward the ATV garage, and when they came to a bog, he let her climb on his back, then carried her, the cooler, and rolled-up blanket through the muck like he didn't mind mud on his jeans. And all the while, he talked about his and Weston's plans for this place. She loved the sound of Ryder's deep, rich voice when he was excited like this.

He backed out a couple of quads and showed her how to use the smaller of the two. Then he strapped the cooler on the back of his with bungie cords and pulled a wide circle, his face in an animated smile as he talked, his eyes following her. Everything slowed, and the moment dragged blissfully on. Ryder had put on a baseball cap backward, and his thin, white V-neck T-shirt was splattered with mud and dirt from the work he'd been doing before she'd shown up. His jeans were old and threadbare at the knees, and his giant work boots were muddy as he shifted gears on his ATV. His lips moved in slow motion with the words he spoke to her, and his blue eyes sparked with happiness.

She loved him.

That's what this joyous buzzing feeling in her middle was. She'd fallen that deep already.

Time resumed its natural rhythm, and Lexi pressed the throttle, easing her quad into the tracks Ryder had made. After a few minutes of getting used to it, her confidence grew and she felt comfortable enough to speed up. Ryder grinned over his shoulder in a challenge and hit the gas.

His laughter echoed through the woods and flooded her heart as she raced after him, her lungs burning with how hard she was laughing. He led her through mud puddles and around tree stumps. He led her past brambles and brush, up hills and through gently rolling creeks.

This place was beautiful. Ryder was building a business in an enchanted wood, and she had no doubt that tourists would fall in love with the adventure he and Wes would lead them on. Up and up, they climbed sloping hills until Ryder pulled to a stop in a clearing. He cut the engine, hopped off his quad, showed her how to turn hers off, and then helped her down. Her shoes and calves were splattered with dark mud, but she couldn't find it in herself to care. Ryder didn't seem like a man who needed his woman perfect.

After Ryder unstrapped the cooler, he pulled Lexi by the hand toward an old, uprooted tree lying on its side. "You ready?" he asked, but the humor had faded from his face.

Her opinion of this place mattered to him.

"Is it special?" she asked.

"It's where I come when everything gets too heavy."

His hand went gentle under hers as he helped her over the log. And when she was settled on the ground, she looked up and gasped in awe. The Smoky Mountains stretched on and on in front of them, green waves jutting up gracefully from the earth. The sky above was a rich color of blue, just like Ryder's eyes. Wisps of white clouds painted the blue canvas in hurried brush strokes.

"Oh Ryder, it's amazing." She shouldn't ask, because it might ruin the moment, but she had to know exactly where she stood with him. "Have you showed this to anyone else?"

When he shook his head, his eyes were raw and honest. "Haven't wanted to share it with anyone but you."

Her eyes prickled with emotion, and she jerked her gaze back to the incredible scenery and blinked rapidly. "I think you're my favorite person," she whispered, too chicken to look at him.

There was a smile in his voice when he said, "Good."

Ryder sat on the ground in front of the log and

began pulling out their lunch. Lexi sat on the log behind Ryder and leaned on him, hugging his shoulders. He laughed and pulled off his baseball cap, then put it on her head. It was too big and drooped down, which made her laugh. Pulling the rim backward, she rested her chin on his shoulder and opened her mouth for the bite of catfish he offered her on a plastic fork.

And as he chatted on easily, he relaxed back against her and fed them both a bite at a time as if they'd known each other forever. And it felt like they had. As she listened to stories about when he was a kid and the trouble he'd found with his friends, she fell even harder for him.

Because of Ryder, she'd lived more in the past week than she had in years. She'd laughed and smiled more than she could remember, and the way she felt about him now was like first love. The kind that stuck with a heart forever. The kind that was the starting point to deep happiness.

She wasn't saying the words to him, but she felt the butterflies and the heart flutters that said she was in deep.

And if the genuine smile on his lips, the booming

laughter, and the constant affectionate pets were anything to go by, Ryder was diving in deep with her, too.

Nothing in her entire life had been as exciting as thinking about the endless possibilities of a future with the quick-witted, dirty-talking, endearingly sweet Air Ryder.

SEVEN

"Favorite color?" Ryder asked, stroking her hair.

Lexi had her head resting on his stomach as they stared up into the tall forest canopy. Ryder had spread out the blanket on thick grass, so her back was nice and comfy right now. Crossing her legs at the ankles, she lifted her hand into the air. She spread out her fingers under the speckles of sunlight that filtered through the trees. Now she looked as freckled as Ryder. "Gold." She wouldn't tell him it used to be purple, or that her new favorite was because of Ryder's eye color when he got riled up, but from his soft chuckle, she thought maybe he knew.

"Yours?" she asked.

Ryder rested his arm under his head and ran his

other fingers through her hair again. "Orange, but for a silly reason."

"Tell me."

"In the Boarlanders, I have a crew member who is kind of like an uncle to me."

"What's his name?" She wanted to know every single thing about Ryder.

"Bash. He's real simple in how he talks and thinks, but he's a beast at handling crew finances. He just has a head for numbers, you know? They make sense to him. Anyway, he's a good man, completely devoted to his mate, has three daughters who think he hung the moon because he was just so damn good and natural at taking care of his girls. I looked up to him a lot when I was growing up, and his favorite color was orange. Not bright orange, but like sunset orange. I like orange because Bash was so excited about the color when I was growing up."

She rolled her head on his stomach and couldn't help her mushy smile. Sweet, loyal man.

"My turn," he said in that deep, rich voice of his. "You ever been arrested?"

"No! Wait, maybe once."

"Maybe? Criminal."

"My friends and I got caught spray-painting maroon devils down the middle of Main Street after a big playoff game. We got busted at three in the morning and had to sit in a cop car while the officer called our parents. I didn't go to jail, though, so does it count?"

"Counts. Did you wear handcuffs?" Ryder asked, arching his eyebrows suggestively.

"No, perv, now you go. Have you ever been arrested?"

"Uuuh, yes."

"Oh God, why am I not surprised?" she said with a laugh.

"After the shifter rights vote, the police cracked down on us hard. I got taken in a few times for public indecency."

"You were streaking?"

"No, my Changes aren't magic. They're scientific, so my clothes don't just magically appear when I Change back to my human form."

"Oooh, now I get it. You would be seen after a Change?"

"Yup. And then there was that whole painting a giant penis on the water tower incident that definitely got me taken in. I saw the police lights and made like an owl and got the fuck out of there, but I'd left my clothes behind and my wallet was in the back pocket of my jeans. They came and picked me up in the middle of the night and, oh, my dad was pissed. He laughs hard about it now, tells that story every damn holiday, but when the police told him what I'd done, his face turned red like a tomato and his veins popped out of his forehead. I almost wanted them to keep me in jail so I didn't have to go back and face his wrath. I had to hand paint the entire tower to cover up the dick, and I was grounded all senior year."

Lexi's stomach shook with her laughter, and she rolled over on her side to better see him. "I bet you were a little monster to raise."

"I was for sure. My mom always said she hoped I had a kid who is just like me so I can see how much her and Mason went through raising me. The woman's tryin' to curse me, I swear. She loves it, though. She can't stop laughing when her and Mason get to swapping stories about me. My sisters were super easy for them to raise. Straight A students, good girls, and they were both born piglets so no flight feathers for them. They like to give me hell for how bad I was, but really, I just made it to where they could get away with anything. My parents were always saying, 'Well, at least it's not as bad as when Ryder did *this*.'"

Lexi climbed over him, laid down on his stomach, and rested her forearms under her chin. His heartbeat picked up as she smiled at him. "Your social media accounts scare me."

"Why?" he asked, a slight frown marring his red eyebrows.

"Because you have hundreds of thousands of followers on each of your accounts. So many women who would just throw themselves at you. And your posts are all funny and engaging. And you post all the half-naked pictures and you look so good, but also really out of my league."

Ryder drew his arm farther under his head, propping up his neck. He stroked his other fingertips down her spine. "The accounts are just for attention." Well, at least he was honest. "I started them between girlfriends when I was just feeling like shit and wanted an outlet. People responded online, and at first it was fulfilling, you know? All this positive attention from strangers. It got me out of my funk.

But after a while, it just felt like…I dunno. Like the fans were pretend, and the things they said didn't really touch me anymore. They weren't real. None of it was. When I was a kid, Weston's dad said that someday everyone would know my name as Air Ryder." He frowned thoughtfully. "I'm pretty sure he didn't think I would get famous for nudie pics and dirty jokes though."

That sounded like a heavy burden—knowing from childhood that his fate was to be well-known. Lexi would've rebelled against a destiny like that and gone into hiding, but Ryder had embraced it and shouldered the pressure. He was even stronger than she'd realized.

"I like you," she blurted out.

Ryder brushed her hair over to the side and began stroking down her spine again, his eyes averted. "What do you mean by that?"

"I mean I like the real you. The social media accounts? I read through your posts for two hours and didn't feel like I knew you any better. I already thought you were funny and that your body was incredible, but I adore you when you're like this even more. I like the serious parts, the humble parts, and the way you don't really take yourself seriously like you try to convince the world you do. I like all the extra stuff beyond the one-liners and the muscles."

In the middle of her heartfelt admission, Ryder's eyes had drifted to her cleavage and glazed over.

Lexi swatted his shoulder. "Are you listening? I'm bearing my soul here!"

"Yes, I'm listening! But your tits are all mashed against me, and they're soft as fuck. I have a boner, *obviously*, and if you could just say that all again while you're rubbing your pelvis against mine, that would be great."

"Ridiculous man," she complained, trying to hide her grin. "I just told you something hard, so now it's your turn."

"I'm an open book. Nothing is hard."

The smile dipped from her lips as she remembered the way he'd looked mid-panic-attack when she'd pulled up. "What was wrong with you earlier? What were you thinking about?"

Ryder's eyes dimmed, and slowly he shook his head, denying her an answer.

She shouldn't feel so slapped by his rejection, but he'd just shut her out of something big. Desperate to be let in behind the walls he'd so obviously built up, she whispered, "Please."

Ryder let off a low, humming sound in his throat that sounded animalistic and pissed off all at once. His eyes sparked like gold flames in the second before he ripped his gaze away from her and gave his attention to the woods. The air felt heavier now, harder to breathe somehow, and chills blasted up her skin. Her instincts screamed to move away from him, but she felt like she was close to something. Close to peeking into his soul, perhaps, so she froze on top of him instead, careful not to move a single muscle.

Ryder dragged in a quick breath, as though his chest was constricting his lungs. "My real dad was an asshole, and sometimes I still let him in my head. I'm thirty years old, haven't seen or heard from him since I was five, and I was raised by the best step-dad my mom could've found for me. So it's super fucked up that I still think about my real dad because it's disrespectful to Mason."

"Why did he leave?"

Ryder sat up suddenly and positioned her over his lap, hugged her against him so hard it was even more difficult to breathe. He hid his face from her, buried it against her neck. "Lexi, I don't want to talk about this. Please just drop this."

"Okay," she whispered, because this conversation wasn't helping Ryder. It was hurting him. She could tell from the way his arms shook around her ribcage. Nothing in her wanted to ruin this perfect day. If he wasn't ready to share this part with her, it was okay.

So she admitted something she hated thinking about as a reward for him giving her that much. "You know when I told you about my ex?"

"Yeah." His voice sounded too low, too rough.

"And about how he cheated on me?"

"Yeah."

"He told me the day before we were supposed to get married, right before our rehearsal dinner."

Ryder's limbs stopped shaking, and he hugged her hard. Lexi gasped at how strong he was, and he released her in a rush. Leaning back on locked arms, he cast his brightly-colored gaze off to the side and said carefully, "Tell me."

"I had my wedding gown all steam cleaned and ready, hanging from the top of my closet door. The bridal luncheon was done, I had all the favors, flower arrangements, caterers, the venue, everything already paid for. My mom and I didn't really get along, but she came around for the wedding planning and supported me one hundred percent. Everything was just as I had dreamed of as a little girl. It was perfect." Her eyes burned with tears she refused to shed, so she blinked hard and continued. "Everything was perfect except the person I'd chosen to spend the rest of my life with. Blake had gotten his secret girlfriend pregnant, and he was starting a family with her instead of me. I. Was. Devastated. And instead of helping me deal with the mess he'd made, he took her on our honeymoon—the one I'd paid for—while I had to cancel everything, send the gifts back, and tell everyone the wedding was off. That's the thing I hate talking about. Hate it. My family doesn't even mention Blake or what happened anymore because I shut down for a year afterward. I hated everything and everyone, and I felt like I couldn't trust people anymore. I'm coming out of it and finding myself again, but thinking about what happened makes me feel like I'm standing on the edge of a cliff and the wind has kicked up. It makes me feel like I could so easily fall back into the hole Blake created." She cupped Ryder's cheeks and dragged his glowing gold gaze back to hers. "So, you see, I've loved someone more than they loved me before, too, and I understand you don't want to talk about ghosts. I still like you the same."

Ryder winced in the instant before his lips crashed onto hers. His hands gripped her waist desperately, and she got it. Emotion was burning her up, too. This kiss banished thoughts of Blake, and she hoped with her whole heart it banished thoughts of Ryder's asshole biological father, too. She didn't know what his father had done to the man she loved, but she hated his real dad for putting darkness inside a creature of the light. Ryder was a man who could make a person feel incredible with a joke or a smile, but the man who was supposed to love him the most had hurt him as a kid. He'd hurt him so badly Ryder still wrestled with the demons conjured by that rejection.

She wanted to make him feel better, and to make herself feel better, too, so she eased out of their kiss just enough to pull her tank top over her head. Without a moment of hesitation, Ryder pulled his shirt off and unsnapped her bra with a competent snap of his fingers. He yanked the loose bra from her arms. She thought he would stare, drink her in, but he did something better. Ryder pulled her immediately against his chest and exhaled a shaky breath. He rocked them, as if the feeling of her bare skin against his was a feeling he'd waited for his whole life.

He was shattering her heart with his tenderness. She'd imagined intimacy with the dirty-mouthed, sexually-charged Air Ryder would be quick and hard, but he was lips melding onto hers, soft strokes against her skin, racing heartbeats, and a soft sound in his throat that was nothing shy of content.

This felt huge—like her first time.

She rolled her hips against his, and he cupped the back of her head, fingers intertwined in her long hair as he pressed his tongue past her lips and tasted her gently. His other arm was strong and steady on her back, drawing her close, keeping her sensitive breasts pressed against his rock hard chest.

God, she loved this. Loved being this close to him. His hard erection was pressed just right against the seam of her jeans, and as he rolled his hips for the first time, she gasped at how perfect the friction was between her legs. Heat pulsed into her chest, and she let off a tiny pained sound at the shock of it. Ryder flinched away, as though he'd felt it, too, and suddenly, the wind picked up, lifting her tresses from her shoulders. He stared at her as if he was really seeing her for the first time.

A baffled smile stretched his lips. In a barely audible whisper, he said, "You felt that...right?"

Lexi pressed her hand over her chest to see if her skin was hotter there. "Yeah," she murmured.

And now Ryder's mouth was on her neck as he squeezed her. He sucked hard, drawing a sharp gasp from her lips at the erotic combination of pain and pleasure. His teeth grazed her, and she rocked onto him helplessly. Fingers fumbling, she unsnapped his jeans and made a pathetic attempt to shove his pants down his hips. Ryder chuckled against her throat and helped her out by unsheathing himself. He pushed his jeans down his legs until they were in the grass beside the blanket. "Your turn," he murmured, then sucked hard again.

"You're going to give me hickeys," she accused as she stood and unbuttoned her jean shorts.

"Mmm," he grunted, swatting away her hands. "Owls don't do claiming marks. Don't mean I want to leave you completely unmarked, though." He slid her shorts down her legs slowly. She'd already taken off her shoes when they'd laid out the blanket, so there was nothing to trip him up from removing them completely and tossing them with his on the forest floor.

"Mmm hmm, yep," she murmured as she stared down at his huge dick, jutting out like a damn tree branch between his legs. The head of his cock was swollen and capped by a drop of moisture. "Mark me. Yep. Hickey," she said, trying to convince him she'd been listening, but whoa fuck, she couldn't remember how to use her words.

Ryder's eyes were gold and stunning as the sunlight hit them just right. They raked down her body, hitting all the hot spots as a feral smile took his face. She'd never seen a man look this hungry in her life, and he was giving that look to her. Normally, she would've been embarrassed about being laid bare and vulnerable in front of a man like this, but it was impossible not to feel like a complete goddess when Ryder was looking at her like this.

She moved to straddle his hips and get this show on the road, but he stopped her with an iron grip on her waist, and before she knew what was happening, he buried his face between her legs and ran his tongue up her wet slit.

Her legs went—just boom—knees gave out, but Ryder was holding her in place, supporting her completely now as he sucked gently on her clit.

God, this should be mortifying. She was out in the woods, in broad daylight, and when she looked down, both of her nipples were drawn up to tight little buds, and Ryder's red hair was shining gold between her legs. But it was pretty damn hard to focus on how embarrassed she should be when he was laving his tongue against her and easing her toward release with every gentle suck on her sensitive nub.

Legs shaking, Lexi let off a helpless noise as the pressure built in her middle. Running her hands through his hair, she closed her eyes against the saturated sunlight and relaxed into his affection. Three more licks, and she was desperate for his tongue to be inside of her because orgasm was coming in hard and fast.

"Ryder," she pleaded.

She swore she could feel him smile against her,

the tease. She gripped his hair harder, pulled him closer, couldn't help herself because she was gone now. And right before she lost it completely, Ryder adjusted his angle and plunged his tongue deep into her. The first pulse of ecstasy exploded around his tongue, but he wasn't done. As she threw her head back and cried out, Ryder stroked into her over and over, drawing out every single aftershock until her legs were numb and she was a jumble of incoherent thoughts.

Ryder eased her down with his strong hands on her waist, kissing her stomach, her belly button, the line between her ribs. Each breast got a hard suck before he allowed her to finally settle on his lap. And then he was kissing her lips, and she could taste herself. With anyone else, that would've been strange, but with Ryder, it was just natural. And he didn't seem to care at all. In fact, he kept smiling against her lips, and once, he chuckled.

She pressed herself against his erection and glared. "You aren't supposed to laugh during sex."

"False. If you aren't having fun, you're doing somethin' wrong."

She giggled and rested her forehead against his

shoulder and rolled her head back and forth slowly. "As long as you aren't laughing *at* me."

Ryder leaned forward, bit her neck, and then tickled her ribs until she was squirming and laughing. "Stop, stop, stop," she crowed. "You're turning me off."

"First off, I can hear lies, and second"—he dragged his fingertips up her wet folds, his lips smiling against hers—"you sure as fuck don't feel turned off."

She let off a low, gleeful laugh and nipped his bottom lip. Cheeky man, but maybe he had a point. She'd never had this much fun with a man during intimacy. It had always been wham, bam, thank ya ma'am, but Ryder had just made sure she came before he even took his own pleasure. And he was making laughter a natural part of sex with him. Fuck yes to all of this.

Feeling bold, Lexi kissed down his chest, bit his nipples gently, then went lower and lower. With a grin, she bit his hip, and then his other, and reveled in the fact that every time her teeth grazed his skin, he rolled his hips and relaxed his legs a little more. And when she gripped him at the base of his dick and looked up to tease him, she was stunned at how striking her man was. Gold eyes locked on her like she was the most beautiful thing he'd ever seen, the corners of his lips lifted in an adoring smile, his freckles stark against his fair skin, his muscles on his shoulders, pecs, and abs flexed to perfection. How had she gotten lucky enough to land in this moment with him?

Humor leaving her, she focused on making him feel good, just like he'd done for her. She slid her lips over the head of his cock and sighed happily as he gripped her hair and groaned. He was noisy when she did something he liked, and there was something infinitely sexy about that. Ryder bent one of his knees beside her, widened his legs, and rocked his hips the next time she took him. He was big, so she had to use her hand to help, but he didn't seem to mind. And the smoother she got with her rhythm, the more he relaxed. Eventually he started panting, his abs flexing with every breath. He rolled his head back and his grip tightened in her hair, as if he was getting close, but he was still gentle with her.

He blew out three sharp breaths and murmured in a panicked tone, "Stop, stop."

For an instant, she thought she was doing something wrong, but when she eased off him to ask, he flipped her over on her back so fast, her stomach dipped. Stunned at the strength and speed he'd been hiding, her body froze in defensiveness, but Ryder didn't seem to notice. He lowered his body to hers and kissed her lips. He was so heavy, so solid, so warm. So perfect molded to her as though he was made to fit into the cradle of her hips.

He curved his body, and she could feel it—the flex of his abs against her soft stomach, the racing of his heart, the swollen head of his cock pressing against her entrance. And all the defensiveness melted from her body. She'd never wanted anything more than this moment of connection with Ryder.

She rolled her hips invitingly in a silent plea. Ryder angled his head and thrust his tongue into her mouth, then slid into her slowly. Then out, and the next time he rolled forward, he buried himself deeper.

She was stretching with him, moving with him, sheathing him, and damn, it felt so good to be this close. The second he went deep enough that he bumped her clit, the pressure he'd conjured earlier was back and more intense. He moved in and out of her with a slick sound, and she arched her back against the blanket, desperate to be even closer to his warmth. The strange hot sensation in her chest was back, and Ryder grunted against her neck where he was sucking on her skin. It grew hotter with every stroke Ryder pushed into her, but it wasn't painful. Just there. Ryder bucked faster now, harder. Spreading his knees wider, he pushed her legs farther apart and pounded into her, gripping the back of her hair, holding her back to keep her pressed tightly against him. He rested his forehead on hers. His teeth were gritted, his eyes gold, and he was as lost as she was now. She fucking loved him like this. Ryder's skin slapped against hers as he thrust into her, and now she couldn't help herself.

"Yes, harder!" she cried, closing her eyes because suddenly, the sunlight was too damn bright. There was so much heat in her chest.

She clawed at his back and shoulders, didn't care if she broke his skin. If he was going to leave hickeys, she was going to leave him all clawed up.

"Fuck, Lexi!" he gritted out, holding her even tighter.

So fast and hard, and the pressure and heat were all too much. Lexi shattered from the inside out, screaming out his name as her orgasm blasted through her. On the second pulse, the heat turned to fire as Ryder slammed into her hard and throbbed inside of her. He groaned with every erratic thrust into her now as shot after shot of wet warmth pulsated into her. Ryder gasped and clutched at his chest as if he felt the hot poker she did. Clenching his teeth and squeezing his eyes tightly closed, he murmured her name again in a raspy voice. His rhythm changed and slowed as their orgasms pounded on.

And when at last he leaned down and drank her lips softly, the pain in her chest was replaced with a fluttering, happy feeling. Ryder sipped at her for minutes, or maybe hours, she didn't know. Lexi lost all sense of time as he pulled her over on her side and held her close, wrapped his arms around her and made her feel so safe as he kissed on and on.

Completely sated, Lexi eased back and smiled emotionally at him.

Ryder's chronic smile was gone, and in its place was a tender expression as he tucked her hair behind her ear. Lexi smoothed the slight frown from his eyebrows, ran her fingertips down his cheek, down his neck, and hesitated at a small scar under his collar bone. It was raised and silver, but perfectly straight, as if it had been done on purpose.

"What's this?" she whispered, resting her cheek on his outstretched arm to better see him.

"Owls don't mark each other, but boars mark the people who are theirs. Mason gave my mom two cuts when I was five, claiming her. My dad had just signed away parental rights, and I wanted Mason to keep me so bad. He was hurt in a boar war in Damon's Mountains, and the crews thought he wouldn't make it. I remember just sitting at the foot of his bed and crying because I wanted him to stay." A thin rim of moisture lined Ryder's eyes, but he kept his gold gaze steady on her. "I'd made up my mind that no matter what, I was his boy. So I took a sharp stick and cut a mark into my skin. It was too shallow, and the scar wouldn't take because of my shifter healing. So when Mason finally woke up, my mom told me I had to tell him what I'd done so he could get onto me for hurting myself. But instead of punishing me, he knelt down in front of me, pulled his pocket knife from his back pocket, and gave me one mark. And he hugged me up and told me I was his." Ryder swallowed hard. "And that's why I don't like to talk about my real dad. I have no right to mourn. Mason might not be blood-related to me, but he's my dad."

So incredibly thankful that he'd shared that with her, Lexi scooted closer and hugged Ryder close. She'd loved him before that admission, but now her heart belonged to him completely.

"Lexi?" he murmured against her ear.

"Yeah?"

He pressed his lips to her cheek, let the kiss linger there before he whispered, "I think you're what I've always been looking for."

EIGHT

Ryder blew out a harsh breath and forced himself to stop shaking his leg under the table. Serena had texted him twice this morning, promising to let him see Dottie for their Tuesday call. Head games. It was like she sensed he was on the mend after the wreckage she'd turned his life into, so now she was back to sink her claws in deeper. Wouldn't work, though. His heart belonged to Lexi now.

Still, he missed Dottie so fucking badly.

It was time to call Serena, but he couldn't make himself hit the connect button on his laptop. The thought of even talking to his ex made his stomach feel like he'd eaten a dozen gas station burritos. This was the moment he had to choose between hanging onto Dottie, or letting her go and cutting ties with the woman who'd tried to destroy him.

Alana sat across the table from him, straightened her bright pink Alana's Coffee & Sweets apron, and lifted her gold eyes to him.

"You smell like fur," he gritted out. She was a brawler. If he was in his owl form right now, she would have every feather on his body puffed up defensively.

"As your second best friend, I don't want you to call Serena. That woman is poison, Air Ryder. I like Lexi for you instead." Whoo, full nick-name. Alana was serious.

Ryder pulled up Serena's messages and pushed his phone across the table.

Alana's deep scar on her lip stretched as she read the messages out loud. "You there? I have been thinking a lot about everything and how much I hurt you. I'm sorry, Ry-Ry. I just want you to come back to me so I can make it up to you. I'll spend the rest of my life making you happy. Me, you, and Dottie can be a family again. To show you I'm serious, I promise I'll let you talk to Dottie today when you call. I love you, Ry-Ry." Alana gagged and scrunched up her face. She tucked a fallen curl behind her ear, settled the phone on the table, and leveled him with a look. "You want to know what I think?"

"You'll tell me even if I say no."

"Yep. I think bitch-face saw you post about how happy you are on your social media. She's following you, Ryder. She's one of those women who doesn't really want you but wants you chasing her. I'm sorry about Dottie, but don't call Serena. Don't do it."

"I wasn't considering a call to rekindle things, Alana. Lexi has me now. I wanted to say goodbye to Dottie. I just have a feeling this is my last chance to see my dog, you know?"

"Ryder, you love her too hard."

"What do you mean?"

"I mean when you pick something, you give it your whole heart. You did that with Dottie, I know. But this is one of those things where you need to stop lookin' back and realize what you have in front of you."

"Lexi."

"Yeah, and Sprinkles and your crew, your friends, your family. You want everyone you love gathered close for always, but you have no control over Dottie, and seeing her one last time isn't going to help anything. It's going to give Serena motivation to keep you under her thumb." Alana stood up and ruffled his hair, shoved his head. "I've known Lexi for a long time. We went to middle school and high school together, and she was always steady. She was kind to everyone. Lexi is a good woman who would never treat you like Serena has done. Covet her, Ryder. Don't call your ex."

Alana sauntered off behind the display case of pastries to help a customer, and Ryder leaned back on the bench seat. She was right. Saying goodbye to Dottie wasn't worth hurting Lexi over. Not after the day they'd spent together. Not after she'd put this warm, happy feeling into his chest. He'd rather sever his own arm than hurt her.

Lexi had showed him something he thought no one would ever be able to. She showed him what a monster Serena had been, and not just for cheating on him. For draining his savings and using his dog as leverage. How had he put up with that shit for so long?

Because you wanted the bond so badly.

Thank God for Lexi showing him what a healthy

relationship could be.

She'd opened his eyes to so much, and now he wanted to get his shit together more than ever before. He wanted to get his business off the ground and save money for a family. He wanted to fix the hole in his middle so she would never have to question if she was enough to make him happy.

Ryder wanted to give her everything.

His computer chirped, and he dragged his gaze to the glowing screen. Serena was calling. Seeing his dog one last time was right there, right at the click of a button. All he had to do was accept, but if he did this, it would hurt Lexi. A vision of betrayal in her eyes flashed across his mind, and he winced away from the thought. He couldn't do this. He loved Lexi. Real love, not the forced kind.

Ryder slammed his computer closed and grabbed his cell phone. He scrolled through the last couple of pictures he'd taken until he came to his favorite of Lexi.

He'd taken it after they'd slept together out in the woods the other day. She'd just gotten dressed, and she was sitting with her back to him, arms wrapped around her drawn-up knees as she overlooked his favorite view—the one he hadn't shared with anyone else. Her long, black hair was hanging in silken waves down her back, and he'd planned on sneaking a picture of her, just like that. But right before he'd taken the picture, she'd turned and given him such a beautiful look over her shoulder. Her green eyes were bright and happy, and a stunning smile stretched her lips. Shocked by her beauty, he'd rushed the picture, but it had somehow still come out perfectly clear. His girl and his favorite view, surrounded by his favorite woods, and this was now his favorite picture of all time.

Alana had been right about him looking to the future and appreciating what he had.

Ryder had never posted about who he was dating on his accounts. They were for fun, and his followers had come to expect half naked pictures and jokes from him. But right now, he wanted to shout to the world that Lexi had come in and dumped his life upside down in the best way. On each account, he posted the picture of his beautiful Lexi with the caption:

I searched the world and finally found her.

#sexylexi #backoffboys #allmine #hoohoo #pussyryder #sheisgoingtokillmeforpostingthis #writediedhappyonmytombstone

His notifications started going crazy with the likes and comments, but he wasn't in the mood to absorb the attention right now. All he wanted to do was call Lexi and hear her voice.

He tucked his computer under his arm and made his way behind the counter. Alana was helping a couple choose pastries, but he snuck into the conversation, hugged her shoulders, and kissed her cheek with an animated smack. "I'm bringing a plus one to the wedding, okay?"

Alana giggled and wiped his kiss from her cheek. "Well, ask Lexi nicely then, *Ry-Ry*. Girls like romantic gestures."

He offered Alana a wink and made his way to the door. "I know what I'm doing."

"I feel like that's not a true statement," she called from behind him, but he wasn't up for the banter.

Ryder had a dozen plans rattling around in his head right now and a lot of prep work to do before tonight.

The bell dinged above the door as he exited, and in a rush, he tossed a wave back to Alana, who was watching him through the window as if he'd lost his mind.

But he hadn't. His head had never been so clear.

It was his heart he'd lost.

NINE

"Oh, noooo," Lexi drawled out as she bounced and bumped her way through the gate.

There was a cabin at the edge of a clearing with strange-looking plastic, green shutters and a couple more cabins up the dirt track that wound around jutting black boulders.

She'd definitely thought Ryder lived by himself.

Ryder, Weston, and Aaron sat on the front porch of the first cabin, and up the trail, Alana, Harper, and Wyatt were walking toward her Jeep. Shit, shit, double shit.

Ryder's greeting grin was beaming as she hit the brakes and rocked to a stop next to Ryder's jacked-up, gunmetal gray Chevy pickup. Beer in hand, he jogged down to meet her, but skidded to a stop by the driver's side, his eyes on her cleavage.

"What are you wearing?" he asked, his voice muffled through the door.

Heat blazed up into her cheeks, and she couldn't meet his eyes. She searched the back seat for a jacket or hoodie, or for fuck's sake, a burlap sack would've worked about now. But of course, there was nothing since she'd just cleaned her ride out last night.

Her mortification was infinite, and now the other Bloodrunners were gathering around her Jeep.

Well…there was no help for it. She couldn't just turn around and speed out of here, even if that was exactly what she wanted to do.

Ryder pulled open the door as she unbuckled. Boneless and full of shame, she slid from the seat and clamped her hands in front of her thighs.

"Holy fuck, you look hot!" Ryder crowed. He pointed to each boob in turn. "That's mine and that's mine."

Wes and Aaron were snickering.

"I didn't know the whole crew lived together," Lexi choked out. "I thought you lived alone."

"That's okay, nobody minds you dressed up as

a…" Realization struck Ryder's face like lightning. "Is this for me because of what I said the other day?"

"What did you say?" Harper asked, biting her lip to hold back a smile. She was failing.

Lexi wanted to crawl in a hole and never come out. "Ryder said he always had this fantasy of fucking a Wild West saloon girl."

Aaron doubled over and laughed so loud it echoed across the mountains, but Alana shoved hard, and he almost fell over. Wes was staring at Lexi's tits, pushed up to her chin with the red silk corset lined in black lace. Ryder looked so damn gleeful Lexi wanted to slap him.

"This is your fault!" she snapped. "You told me to dress like this."

"I assure you I did not. I would remember. I said 'dress for the woods.'"

"Oh. Shit," Lexi muttered. "Well…" She pulled down the tiny skirt to cover up her fishnet clad thighs a little better. "That makes more sense then."

"What did you think I said?"

Her cheeks caught fire. She cleared her throat delicately and muttered, "I thought you said 'dress for wood.'"

Wyatt and Aaron weren't even trying to stifle their laughter now, Wes was still staring at her fucking tits, and Ryder was doubled over cackling and stomping his feet, spilling his beer all over the grass.

Alana looked impressed, though, and she punched out through her giggles, "Girl, at least you're working it. You came to get your man."

"He's not getting anything now," Lexi grumbled.

Harper shoved Wes's head, and he came out of his tit-trance, but just barely.

"I have some clothes you can borrow if you want," the Bloodrunner alpha offered. "You look awesome, but I doubt that will work for where we're going."

"Where *we're* going?" God, she'd really thought when Ryder called earlier, he had a one-on-one date planned for them. Apparently this was a group date, and her mortification somehow deepened.

Ryder picked her up like a sack of flour and tossed her onto his shoulder.

"Ryder!" she squawked as he slapped her bare ass.

"Sorry, y'all. I need at least thirty-three seconds with my girl." Ryder pretended to shoot laser beams from his dick with a couple pelvic thrusts and said in a high pitched voice, "Pew pew."

Lexi struggled, trying to hide her bare body parts from the crew, but Ryder was immovable, the brute.

"Thirty-three seconds, yeah right," Aaron called as Ryder shoved the door to the cabin open. "That would be a record for you, Ryder! One pump wonder!"

"Harper!" Lexi pleaded. "Clothes!"

Ryder shut the door, but she could hear Harper's muffled voice. "I'll bring them to you!"

Ryder strode straight into the bedroom and dumped her unceremoniously on the bed.

"I'm so embarrassed!" She pressed her palms against her burning cheeks to cool them. Ryder was unsnapping his pants like this was really going to happen now, and Lexi opened her mouth to tell him *hell no to all of this*, but movement caught her attention.

When a mouse ran across the wooden floors of the bedroom, Lexi bolted upright on the bed with a horror film scream clawing its way up her throat.

Ryder hunched and covered his ears, and outside Aaron yelled, "Sounds like she saw Ryder's dick!"

More laughter echoed as Lexi inhaled for another scream.

Ryder clapped his hand over her mouth and said, "Woman, stop your screeching! It's a pet mouse!"

"Why would anyone have a rodent as a pet?" she asked, her voice still two octaves too high.

"Because he's fucking awesome. Look at his nuts! They're huge, and he eats food right out of my hand."

Ryder jacked his eyebrows up when she high-kneed it over the bouncy mattress to cower beside him, as far away from the mouse as possible. He peeled her claws from his shirt and left her—left her!—to defend herself. She picked up a pillow and prepared to whack that little sucker if it came any closer.

To her horror, Ryder picked up the little black and white mouse easily and ran his finger gently down the little critter's head. "Lexi, meet Sammy Scrotum, Sammy Scrotes for short. Sammy, this is Sexy Lexi."

Ryder approached her with a teasing grin, and she reared back with the pillow. "Don't you fuckin' dare."

"Come on, pet him. Look how cute he is. Look at

his wittle ears and his wittle whiskers." Ryder scrunched up his nose like a mouse and Lexi bit back a smile. This was not funny.

"Ryder, I don't do mice."

"Ew, me either. That's gross."

Lexi growled at him and backed toward the headboard when he stepped closer.

"Pet him once, and I'll let you suck my pener."

Lexi had to force herself not to laugh. Ryder looked determined, so she asked, "Will it bite me?"

"No! Sammy Scrotum is nice."

"That's a terrible name."

"He likes it. It's a warrior's name. Pet him. Come oooon. Do it. Peer pressure. Give in. Pet him."

Every muscle in her body shaking, she dropped the pillow and stuck her finger out, then squeezed her eyes tightly closed so she could pretend she wasn't actually doing this.

Soft fur touched her fingertip, and she yelped and drew back. She cracked an eye open and tried again. Sammy Scrotum didn't seem to care at all and just went to climbing all over Ryder's open palm, sniffing his little nose and shaking his little whiskers. He was kind of cute, and one of his black spots was shaped like heart, which she really liked.

She brushed her fingertips from his head to his back and down his tail, then flinched away with a proud grin. "I did it."

"You fuckin' did it!" Ryder said, his eyes wide and sparking like blue flames.

As he set the mouse back down on the floor to scurry on its way, Lexi clutched her chest and sighed a gusty exhale. "My heart is going ninety to nothing. It's like hummingbird wings. Feel it!"

Void of hesitation, Ryder grabbed her boob. "Yep, super-fast," he muttered in a tone that said he gave zero fucks about her heartbeat right now and was in it for the teat-fondle.

"Ryder, I'm coming in, stop boning," Harper called from the front door.

"I touched a mouse!" Lexi exclaimed as the dragon-eyed alpha came in with a handful of clothes and a pair of hiking boots on top of the pile.

"You met Sammy?" she asked with a megawatt smile.

"Yes, and he was terrifying and cute, but mostly terrifying."

She giggled and told Ryder, "Fasten your pants,

man."

Ryder threw something small, oval, and chocolate-colored at Harper, who ducked out of the way. Lexi was going to pretend it was anything but a mouse turd, because sanitation.

Ryder disappeared into the bathroom, and the running water of the sink sounded. Harper set out the clothes on the bed and Lexi picked a pair of black skinny jeans and a forest green tank top to go with the hiking boots. The shoes were a size too big but they worked a lot better than the strappy gladiator heels she'd fastened onto her feet when she was dressing in her skanky saloon girl getup.

Ryder came back in smelling like soap as she was lacing the shoes, and without instruction, he took her costume and hung it up in the closet. "For later," he declared.

Harper walked out, calling, "Let's load up. We're burnin' daylight," over her shoulder.

Ryder squared up to Lexi, hands tight on her hips as he sipped her lips. "I liked the costume, but you look good enough to eat out in these jeans."

"It's good enough to eat."

"Hmm?" he asked innocently.

"The saying goes, 'You look good enough to eat.'"

"You want a piggy-back ride, but on my front?"

"No!" she said, swatting him. "Behave tonight and don't embarrass me in front of your friends. I want them to like me."

"Hmm." He frowned. "Can you use the word *behave* in a sentence?" he asked as though he was at a spelling bee.

With an eye roll, Lexi strode out of the bedroom and through the living room toward the front door.

"Can I have the definition?" he asked from behind her, a smile in his voice.

Outside, the Bloodrunners were loading up in Ryder's truck. Aaron and Alana sat in the bed as Wyatt, Harper, and Wes climbed into the back seat.

Ryder pulled the passenger's side door open for her. Unhelpfully, Ryder squeezed her ass as she scrambled in with the grace of a rhino. She was giggling uncontrollably by the time she settled into the seat. Ryder leaned in and kissed her quick, bit her bottom lip, before he pulled away with a wicked grin. "I like tasting your laughs."

Crazy man. As he jogged around the front of the truck, she couldn't help the giant smile that was stretching her lips.

"He makes you happy, doesn't he?" Wes asked in a strange tone.

Lexi twisted in her seat to look back at him and nodded. "I can't remember ever being this happy with someone," she rushed out before Ryder opened his door.

"Good," Wes said, giving his attention to the window.

"Good what?" Ryder asked, buckling in.

"Nothing," Wes murmured.

The smile dipped from Ryder's lips, and he frowned back at the Novak Raven with an upset expression Lexi didn't understand. When she rested her hand on his tensed leg, he relaxed and offered her another smile, but it didn't reach his eyes.

Perhaps he and his best friend were fighting.

It was six o'clock and the early evening shadows were just now lengthening in the Smoky Mountains. Ryder rolled down the windows and turned up a country rock song. After a few minutes of driving a back road, he belted out the first line of the chorus and then looked right at her, daring her to sing along.

She did know the song, but she'd never been

comfortable singing in front of other people. Her voice was reserved for the shower and when she was alone in her Jeep. But then Harper started humming along in the back seat, and Wyatt chimed in off-key. Even Wes sang a word here and there, so fuck it. The second round of the chorus, Lexi murmured the lyrics at normal, conversational volume.

"Yeaaaah!" Ryder said.

He started singing again, even louder, and after she got control of her laughter, Lexi sang, too. And by the time Ryder pulled to a stop in a meadow on the edge of a cliff, they were all belting out the third song, hacking up the lyrics, but no one seemed to care.

It was awesome feeling so comfortable with these people. She'd always wondered how similar shifters were to humans, and after hanging out with them twice now, they were the most normal people she'd ever met.

Everyone started piling out of the truck, but it looked as if they had just stopped at a random bend in the road. "Where are we?"

"I want to show you something." Ryder got out and met her at the front of the truck, then took her hand and led her toward the cliff.

Around her, the Bloodrunners began stripping out of their clothes. Weird. To avoid an eyeful of swinging dicks and bouncing boobs, Lexi aimed her focus on the cliff.

Lexi wasn't afraid of heights, but the cliff dropped straight down, and at the bottom, sharp rocks jutted out of the earth. There was a river some distance off, and the scenery was beautiful, but this was close enough. Lexi backed away from the edge, but when she turned around to ask Ryder what they were doing here, a smattering of pops sounded and a monster grizzly burst from Wyatt, and then a blond one from Aaron. They were so intimidatingly big. They paced around Alana, her Change slower and painful-looking, but when she stood on all fours and roared, she didn't seem to mind the pain. Her fur was a rich, chocolate brown, almost the same as her human skin tone. And though she was smaller than the other grizzlies, Alana still looked ferocious with all those claws and teeth.

Wes leapt off the ground and a giant raven burst from his body. As he circled above, Harper's body rippled and cracked, and then an enormous green and gold dragon exploded from her body. Harper was so big she could curl around the entire Bloodrunner crew.

Lexi had never seen a dragon shift before, had never been this close to one, and she had to hold in a scream as Harper snaked her enormous head toward her. The bears disappeared down a steep trail on the edge of the cliff, and the Novak Raven dove over the ledge. And carefully, Harper stepped over Lexi and Ryder.

In a rush, Ryder grabbed Lexi's hand and lifted it high until her fingertips brushed the golden underbelly scales of the Bloodrunner Dragon.

Amazed at the cold, smooth texture of the dragon scales, Lexi gasped. Harper spread her wings and dove off the cliff.

Lexi followed as close as she dared to the cliff ledge so she could watch the dragon in flight. Harper was grace in motion.

"Do you trust me?" Ryder asked.

Lexi looked at him over her shoulder. He'd stripped out of his clothes, and she was awed by his rippling muscles as he approached. Damn, her man was powerful.

"Of course."

Ryder bunched his muscles. "Good. Don't freak out," he said the moment before the massive white owl ripped out of his skin.

In an instant, he clamped his long, curved talons around her upper arms, and with the beat of his wings, lifted Lexi off the ground and over the edge of the cliff.

Terror seized her as she watched the rocks below coming for her. Ryder had tucked his wings to his body and was dive-bombing them toward the earth. She couldn't scream, couldn't beg for him to stop, couldn't even breathe.

With a resounding *floom*, he stretched his wings and caught the air, arching them away from the ground at such speed, the air was forced into her lungs.

"Ryder!" she gasped, struggling. His talons clutched her arms tighter, the points of his sharp claws digging into the tender undersides. She stopped struggling just to ease the pain. When he slowed and became graceful with his flying, she forced herself to catch her breath and then looked up.

He was staring down at her, his gold eyes round and his pupils so small it made them look even brighter. Even more striking. He was white as snow, but underneath his wings, there were dark specks on his long flight feathers. He was enormous, his wingspan stretching much longer than she'd imagined.

She couldn't believe this was happening. She was flying!

Lexi looked down at the ground far below them. The river snaked through the mountains like a giant serpent, and waves of green painted a gorgeous landscape. Right below, Weston was flying with them, keeping pace.

She laughed breathlessly and held onto Ryder's legs just to steady herself. Her heart in her throat, she arched her neck back and yelled, "Whooooo!"

"Caw!" the Novak Raven called below them.

Ryder belted a powerful screech, and down near the river, Harper roared along with the bears.

As long as Lexi lived, she would remember this moment—her first flight with Air Ryder.

TEN

"I didn't realize how fragile your skin is," Ryder said, his brows furrowed in concentration as he cleaned the small puncture wounds under her arm.

"Worth it," she said breathlessly as she stared up at the sky again. She was just there! Flying!

"What if it gets infected?" Ryder murmured to Wes. "Maybe I should take her to the hospital."

"Stop fussing," she murmured. "I'm fine. They don't even hurt."

"I'm gonna have to make you some kind of arm guards if we do that again."

"I can't believe that just happened," she said gleefully. "Ryder, that was the most incredible thing ever! I mean, it was terrifying at first because I didn't expect it, but then it was exhilarating."

Weston lifted her other arm and brushed a light touch under the cuts. "I think they'll be okay."

"She said she's fine," Alana said from where she was peeling shrimp on a plastic table on the sandy riverbank. "Stop coddling her, or you'll chase her off."

When Ryder immediately dropped her arm, Lexi snorted. Like she would ever leave him. This man had all of her locked down.

She scanned the beach and rolling river rapids, still in awe that a view like this existed down in this valley. There was a generator, and the three trees by the grill were wrapped in outdoor lights. Next to where she stood, there was a long picnic table with carvings of three bears, a dragon, a raven, and an owl. And when she looked closer, there was the beginnings of another carving, right next to the owl. It was human in shape with a few wavy lines of long hair. She frowned and opened her mouth to ask if that was her, but Wes pressed his finger over his lips and shook his head. Huh. A selfish part of her really hoped that was her next to Air Ryder.

Ryder brought her a fruity beer with a swirly straw in it, and then he gestured at the table. There were two simple, shallow wooden bowls full of yellow dandelion flowers. "Those are for you," he said low, ducking his gaze as though he was embarrassed.

He looked so fucking cute right now, his red whiskers on his chiseled jaw two days grown, his eyes the color of the sky, that slight smile that seemed to always sit on his sensual lips. His defined chest and shoulders pressed against a blue T-shirt he'd dug out of a giant plastic container of extra outfits someone had stashed down here. He wore a navy baseball cap on backward, and medium wash jeans hugged his powerful legs. Suddenly desperate to feel his body against hers, Lexi leaned forward and hugged his waist as tight as she could with her puny human arms. "Did you do all this?" she whispered.

"The Bloodrunners helped. I wanted to do something special for you."

"It's so special, and I'm so happy that you give me moments like these, Ryder."

"Can I ask you something big?" he murmured.

Heart pounding, she answered, "Of course. Ask me anything."

Ryder pulled something from his back pocket and dropped to one knee.

Panicked, she asked, "What are you doing?"

He gave her a mushy smile, then popped open the ring box. And inside was a...

Tiny clay penis.

She snorted and reached for it, plucked it from the plush velvet and held it between her finger and her thumb. "Is this a replica of your dick?"

"I made it at the pottery shop in town, just for you."

"It's actual size," Aaron called from by the grill.

"Fuck you, man," Ryder said. He dragged his gaze back to Lexi and tried to keep a straight face when he told her, "Lexi, you're the most beautiful, perfect, funny girl I've ever met. I like how one of your boobs is slightly bigger than the other, and I like the way you snort when you laugh really hard—"

"Ryder," she warned. The crew didn't need to hear all this about her.

"I like how when you brush your teeth, you get toothpaste everywhere and look rabid, but still sexy."

Okay, he was joking now, and she was going to play along. "There is nothing more satisfying than a good minty froth. I like the way you sniff your armpits before we leave the house to make sure you put on deodorant."

His eyes danced. "I gotta smell good for you, baby. I like that one side of your nose goes up higher when you smile."

"Well, I like the way you sniff your food before you eat it."

"Not your food though, Sexy Lexi. You cook good. And I like the way your hair looks like a lion's mane after we make the boing-boing."

Lexi covered her face and shook her head to cover her giggles. "Okay, this has to stop."

"No, don't stop now," Wyatt called. "This is awesome. You're like two weird, malformed peas in a pod. It's like watching a slow-moving train wreck."

"Lexi," Ryder murmured, trying to twist his lips into a serious line again. "Will you do me the honor of accompanying me to Alana and Aaron's wedding?"

Stalling for time so she wouldn't lose it when she answered, Lexi looked at the others who were in different stages of laughter. Finally, she looked down at Ryder with the most serious face she could and said, "I will."

Like a romance movie, he lifted her off her feet and spun her in slow motion until she was dizzy.

"Are we done with these shenanigans?" she asked him.

Ryder set her on her feet and steadied her shoulders when she stumbled. "Only if you keep my tiny ceramic penis in your pocket forever as a good luck charm."

"Fine." She studied it. Ryder had taken the time to paint little veins on it and everything. Geez. She shoved it deep in her jeans' pocket.

"Do you like it?" he asked, and the hopefulness in his voice was so cute.

"I love it."

Ryder swayed them from side to side, then spun her outward in a fancy dance move, and brought her back against his chest. Nonchalantly, he asked, "Do you like me?"

"You know I do."

"Do you get a weird feeling in your chest around me?"

She jerked back. "Yeah. You?"

He grinned and dipped her, kissed her. "Maybe."

"Do you like me?" she asked.

"I gave you my tiny penis," he said, like it should've been obvious.

"I need compliments and declarations," she said primly, sliding her hand in his as he lifted her upright again in the sand.

Ryder looked uncertain for a moment before he buried his face against her neck. And soft as a breath, he whispered, "I love you."

"What?" she said rearing back to look him in the eyes.

"You heard me."

"I want to hear you again when you aren't hiding."

"Why?"

"Because you tease all the dang time, Ryder. I want to know without a doubt that you are being serious. I want you to look me in the eye and tell me."

"Will you say it back?"

"I don't know. Try me."

Ryder let off a little growl and looked around at his crew who all seemed to be suddenly very busy with cooking dinner. He dragged his gaze back to hers, and now his eyes were blue with gold centers, practically glowing in the evening sunlight. "Lexi, I love you."

God, those words and what they did to her. Her

body warmed from the inside out, and she let off a sigh of relief as a strange weight she hadn't realized she was carrying lifted off her shoulders. He felt the same as she did. This thing between them really was as big as she had thought.

Her eyes burning with emotion, she dared to lock on his gaze so he could see the honesty in her eyes when she said the words her heart had been feeling for a while. "I love you, too, Air Ryder."

"Aww!" Alana said, clutching her hands in front of her chest.

"Are you crying?" Ryder asked in a judgmental tone.

"I can't help it," Alana murmured, her eyes glistening. "I've seen you be offensive and obnoxious, but rarely sweet, Ryder."

"Our man-child is growing up," Harper joked from where she was dousing the bowl of shrimp with spicy seasoning.

"I was gonna give y'all some of these fruity beers, but now I'm gonna drink 'em all," he threatened.

Ryder made his way over to the grill and commandeered the tongs away from Aaron, his grin bright as he popped off to his friend. And then the banter started all over again. It was a constant and happy thing in the Bloodrunners. As Lexi watched them laughing and joking as they prepared the big family dinner, she was struck by what she'd found here.

Not only had she found the love of a great man, but he'd given her friends, too.

As if he could hear her mushy thoughts, Ryder gave her a bright grin over his shoulder, then jerked his chin, asking her to join them.

Lexi grabbed a couple fruity beers from the cooler and popped the tops for Alana and Harper. She joined them at the prep table near the grill and helped season the asparagus alongside them.

Ryder gripped her waist and kissed the back of her neck, and she leaned back against him just to feel his warmth. Just to feel that pulsating heat in her chest that always showed up when he was near.

As if he could feel her need to be close, he wrapped his arms around her chest and let his lips linger on her cheek, and she could feel it. The happy smile on his lips that she breathed for.

She'd done her research and knew what was happening between them, and it was huge for both of them.

They weren't using the word yet, but she had no doubt that someday they would.

She was the mate of Air Ryder.

ELEVEN

Sprinkles growled as Sammy Scrotum passed by her princess bed in the corner. He didn't seem to notice as he scampered across the floor with a miniature chocolate chip cookie in his mouth. He disappeared into the bathroom where Ryder talked low to him. "I wouldn't fuck with Princess Sprinkles, Sammy. She's tough."

The tough pooch he was talking about was already asleep again and snoring slightly. She wasn't the best watchdog, but that wasn't why Lexi had fallen for her. Sprinkles had been hit by a car, and Lexi had volunteered to foster her through her rehab and physical therapy. And then she hadn't been able to give her up when the time came.

Lexi was lying on her stomach on the bed in one of Ryder's oversize T-shirts, her head propped on a pillow as she watched Ryder's shadow dance across the floor near the bathroom door. "So if this isn't your house, why are we staying the night here?"

"So when you're screaming my name tonight, Weston doesn't have to listen to it." It was meant to be a joke, she knew, but Ryder's tone was dark.

He strode out of the bathroom naked and crawled across the bed to her, pushed the hem of her sleep shirt up her back. She rolled her eyes closed and sighed as his lips touched her spine. The tickle of his facial scruff was so fucking sexy, a delicious shiver trembled up into her shoulders.

Ryder chuckled against her skin, then ran his tongue a few inches up her lower back. "I got you an anniversary present."

Lexi looked over her shoulder to see if he was teasing, but nope, he was pulling a small, purple gift bag from the floor beside the bed.

Twisting on the bed, she asked, "What is it?"

"Something you've always wanted."

"Awwww." She turned to absolute mush as she tugged the tissue paper off the top to reveal a…thong.

Lexi narrowed her eyes at his big dumb grin. "Something *I* always wanted or something *you* always wanted?"

"Try it on."

"No!" She threw the tiny strip of fabric back in the bag. "They are super uncomfortable. It's like walking around with a wedgie all day."

"I paid ten bucks for that wedgie, miss ma'am, and I want to see your ass cheeks hanging out to greet me."

"Well you paid ten bucks for a damn rubber band so me thinks you got ripped off. I'd rather go commando."

"Deal, I like commando. You're so fucking cute when you're feisty. Makes me just want to bite you."

"Bite me, and I'll bite you back."

"Promise?" Why were his eyes bright gold now? Ryder shoved her panties up her ass crack in a makeshift thong and said, "Good 'nuff."

With a groan, Lexi buried her face against the pillow and tried to hide her laughter.

He swatted her ass, and Lexi flinched. It was one of those quick, stinging ones that went straight from surprise-pain to making her hormones buzz around like a beehive.

"Ryder, if you're gonna spank me like that, you better be prepared to take me hard."

"God, you're the perfect woman. I like you more than I like beer. Look at my handprint!"

Arching her back, Lexi stared over her shoulder at the perfect red outline of his palm. "Do the other side and make me look like a peacock."

Ryder slapped her other cheek and stared at her ass with an expectant grin. Lexi stood on the bed in front of the mirror and cracked up at the handprints on her cheeks, then she strutted around the bed like a proud peacock with her elbows flapping around like wings.

"No, no, you look like a chicken," Ryder punched out between laughs. "Be more majestic."

Lexi jumped up and bounced on her butt against the mattress, then said, "Spill it, smexyboy. Why are we in ten-ten?"

The grin dipped from his face but didn't disappear altogether. Knees on the ground, he leaned his elbows on the bed and gave her lap a significant look. "I need incentive."

Lexi pulled the shirt over her head and dropped

it slowly to the floor, then jiggled her bare boobies for him.

"Maybe just a little more incentive," he murmured, poking a finger at her panties.

"Ryder," she warned.

"I met Mason, my dad, on the steps of an old magic singlewide trailer in the Boarland Mobile Park. And I lived there for a while with him and my mom while they were getting established. Good things happened to me there. My life turned around in ten-ten."

"So you want good things to happen to you here?"

His ruddy eyebrows lowered, and he rested his chin on his forearms. Slowly he shook his head. "I don't care about me anymore, Lex. I want good things to happen to you. All of the mates in Damon's Mountains lived in that old trailer at some point, and it was good luck. There was something special about it. And when we saw this old cabin had the same house number—ten-ten—it felt like a big deal. A sign maybe, I don't know. Harper connected with this place, and so did Alana." Ryder blew out an exhale and admitted in a whisper, "I want to keep you, Lexi."

Heart drumming against her sternum, she murmured, "Ten-ten or no, you already have me."

Intensity flashed through Ryder's gold eyes as he crawled up the bed. When he locked his arms on either side of her face, the muscles in his shoulders bulged. He canted his head in a very animal-like way and raked his hungry gaze down her body, caressing her with a glance.

Gently, she ran the back of her hand down the red scruff on his face. "Next time you get me a present, I want something real. I want a piece of you."

Ryder leaned his cheek against her palm, rolled his eyes closed as though her touch was everything, then pressed his thumb against the tripping pulse in her wrist. He brushed a kiss against her palm and said, "Name it. You can have whatever you want."

"I want a feather," she said softly.

His sexy lips stretched into a surprised smile, and now his pupils were small, just like his owl's had been, the gold color blazing like fire. He was stunning. Without a word, he leaned down and pressed his lips to hers.

She was wrecked. Wrecked for every man who could possibly come after him. Ryder was everything.

He was everywhere. He was the biggest, brightest part of her life now. How fitting that his eyes were the color of sunlight. He was her sun.

Ryder's hand slipped around the back of her neck and squeezed as he lifted, arching her head back to better drink her up. And that man worked her lips until she was breathless and wanting. Until she was sliding her hands up his ribs, pulling him closer. Until she was spreading her knees wider in a silent plea to fill her. To be a part of her because she could never be close enough to him.

The heat in her chest was back, and that used to scare her, but now she thought maybe this was how it was supposed to be. She'd found her person. Despite all the hurt and betrayal of her past, she'd *found* him. Maybe she was supposed to be shattered by Blake so that Ryder would have the chance to put her back together. Maybe Ryder was always meant to be the one who helped her discover the best version of herself. The one who could make her laugh until she cried, who could make her love with everything she had.

Perhaps 1010 wasn't the only magic, as he believed. Perhaps it was also Ryder.

Ryder had come in and awakened her dormant heart, and with every touch, he had opened her further, like a flower meeting the first rays of morning sunlight.

He ran his fingertips down her ribcage, over the swell of her hip, across her thigh, and then cupped her sex. She exhaled softly when he touched her clit. Rocking her hips, she reached down and pressed his hand against her harder, showing him how slow she wanted it.

Ryder pushed his tongue past her lips as he plunged two fingers inside of her. Lexi moaned into his mouth and lost herself completely to his affection. Her mind shut down to everything but his touch. His grip in her hair as he pushed his fingers into her. His warm lips on hers. His taste. His soft groan when she gripped his thick erection.

Slowly, she ran her hand down his long shaft, then pulled him closer to the cradle between her legs. The head of his cock brushed her inner thigh, and she could feel the drop of moisture at the tip as it smeared across her skin. God, she couldn't wait for him to empty himself inside of her.

Gently, she rolled them over until he was

underneath her straddled legs. Ryder's grin turned wicked because he knew. He knew what she was doing. Big dominant shifter, and she was taking control.

And he let her. Ryder pulled his fingers out of her and gripped her waist, lowering her down over his shaft. He was so big, so thick, she had to go slowly as he stretched her. But damn, when he was buried deep and touched her clit, sparks of pleasure shot through her.

As Lexi rocked her hips forward, she clawed her fingers on his chest, scratching him. His grip on her hips tightened, his fingers digging into her skin, but she didn't care. She hoped it bruised. He'd been marking her since they'd met. Hickey's, claw marks under her arms, and now this. He was a rough man who stayed gentle enough to keep pain pleasurable for her, and she loved him even more for it.

Ryder huffed a sharp noise as she rocked against him, and now his teeth were clenched like she was driving him to the edge of his control. Good.

Leaning down, she drew his nipple into her mouth, grazed her teeth against it, sucked hard and Ryder bucked into her deep. He moved her long hair to the other side of her face, probably to watch her. "Faster," he begged in a snarly voice.

Smiling, she bit his nipple and shook her head, then slowed her thrusting, arching her back gracefully with every stroke.

Ryder lifted his knees, curling his body around her, and gripped the back of her neck hard. He pulled her to him and clamped his teeth against her throat, showing her he was in charge. He sucked hard, and she moaned, leaning her head back to give him better access.

She slid almost all the way off, leaving only the head of his cock inside of her before she slid back down again.

"Fffuck," he said shakily. His hand was so tight on the back of her neck, so tight on her waist.

To punish his roughness, she bit his bottom lip hard. Ryder let off a feral humming sound deep in his throat, and when Lexi eased back, his face looked wild. Stunning man, so fucking sexy.

He grabbed her waist and slammed her down on his dick. So deep. Almost too deep, and Lexi gasped at the shock of it. The pressure was building between her legs, tingling with how good this tease was, but

Ryder wasn't having her games anymore. "Woman, get me off or I'm going to lose it and take you up against that wall over there," he growled out.

Well, that actually sounded fun, but she wouldn't last that long. Lexi bucked against him, faster, smoother, unable to keep her cries of ecstasy in her throat any longer.

Ryder was slamming into her now, meeting her blow for blow, and she was done. She screamed his name as orgasm blasted through her body, clenching his dick in quick pulses. Ryder grunted, blazing eyes locked on hers as the first shot of warmth squirted into her. Over and over, he pulsed until his juices streamed out of her. Arms locked on his chest, hair wild and flipped over to the side, boobs bobbing, Lexi twitched over and over until both of their aftershocks were finished.

In no rush to disconnect, she relaxed against his chest and sighed as he petted long strokes down her back with his fingertips. And as the warm sensation in her chest drummed against his, Ryder whispered, "I've never let a woman have control before."

"I'm not just a woman," she murmured.

"No." There was a smile in his voice. "You're my

woman."

Lexi let off a soft laugh and cuddled her arms between their chests. Ryder wrapped his arms around her back and held her tight.

All tucked up and safe, Lexi fell asleep to the song of Ryder's steady heartbeat.

TWELVE

Ryder's phone dinged again, and he cursed himself for not setting it to silent before he fell asleep. It was going to wake up Lexi, and he would straight up rip the prick a new asshole if that happened.

Ding.

Lexi tensed against his chest and made a soft sleep sound. Mother fucker. Carefully, Ryder slid his arm out from under her and rushed to turn the phone to vibrate before it chirped again. He gave zero shits about whoever was texting him right now. If it was important, his crew would've just come over and banged on the door trailer-park style.

An unknown number flashed across the glowing screen, along with the first few words of the message.

Hey Ryder, member me?

Rubbing his eyes to protect them from the bright screen, Ryder sat up on the edge of the bed and opened the message.

Hey Ryder, member me? It's been a long time, but I'm wanting to get to know my boy now. I'm ready. I've missed too much.

Horror filled Ryder's chest as he scrolled down and read the next message.

This is your dad.

And the next.

I mean your real dad because that fuckin' boar don't have any of his blood in you.

And the next.

I want to see you. They prolly turned you against me, but I don't have much time left. Give me a chance to say my apologies and make up for what I done before I leave this world.

The phone felt like a hot coal in his hand so Ryder dropped it as fast as he could. He wanted to retch. How had Robbie even found his number?

"Fuck," Ryder murmured in shock, running his shaky hands through his hair.

The room was spinning as flashback after

flashback pummeled his mind. There was so much he hadn't told Mom about the time he'd spent alone with Robbie. So much Ryder had protected her from, and now the damn devil himself was back for what? Forgiveness.

Fuck that shit.

He couldn't breathe. His throat was tightening, and he would suffocate alone here in the dark. Clutching at his chest, Ryder looked around the room in desperation. Where the fuck was he? This wasn't his cabin.

"Babe?"

A hand touched his back, and Ryder flinched away.

"Ryder, what's wrong?"

"Ten-ten," he murmured. He was in 1010 with Lexi. That was her pretty voice full of concern. He was okay. He just needed to breathe. *Breathe, breathe, breathe. She can't see you like this. Keep her.*

He blew out a shaky breath and forced his shoulders to relax. It was all for show. His insides felt like he'd just ripped the pin out of a grenade and swallowed it. *Keep her.*

Lexi's hands were on him now, rubbing up his

shoulders, trying to soothe him, but it wouldn't fix the crack in his soul. The deep, dark one that he'd patched up with a single strip of duct tape so he could appear to be normal on the outside.

Fuckin' Robbie.

Keep her.

"It was a bad dream." His voice came out too low, too gravelly, too panicked. He cleared his throat. "It's okay. Everything's okay."

What did he want from Ryder? To fuck up the next thirty years of his life? He'd just gotten Lexi, and now Robbie was going to fuck it up. *Not if you don't let him.*

The ghost-sound of a resounding slap echoed through the room. *You fuckin' little freak!*

Ryder closed his eyes against the vitriol in Robbie's voice.

Desperate to escape his head, Ryder rounded on Lexi. He shouldn't do this. Shouldn't. He should let her go back to sleep so Robbie's evil reach didn't touch her through Ryder, but he couldn't stop himself. He wanted out of his head, and Lexi could make it all better.

Ryder pulled her close and covered her mouth

with his. When he plunged his tongue deeply into her mouth, she gasped. *Keep her.*

But then she gave him salvation. She didn't push him away and tell him to get his shit together. Lexi—his Lexi—slid her arms around his neck and pulled him closer. And as if she knew what he needed, she straddled his hips and rocked against his half-mast erection. That did it. He hardened by the second, and she was already wet. She would be so fuckin' tight right now because he wasn't taking the time to prepare her, but fuck it. He needed her wrapped around his dick now. He needed to lose his mind.

Ryder flipped her over onto her hands and knees and gripped her hips as he pushed into her. Stroke one, and the tension was already easing from his shoulders. She cried out as he pushed into her again, and as he froze, thinking he'd hurt her, she gasped out, "Harder!"

Fuck, she was saving him, and she didn't even know it.

Ryder reared back and thrust into her again, buried himself balls deep inside her. He didn't stop but pummeled her until she was screaming his name, touching herself, rubbing her own clit. His balls clenched as he yelled out and shot his load into her. He wanted every creamy drop he had to give inside of Lexi right now. He wanted her messy. He wanted it running down her thighs and pooling on the bed sheets. He wanted her to smell like him, salty and rutting.

Lexi came hard, clenching his dick in quick, pulsing release as she moaned over and over. Good mate, knowing what he needed.

Like she had no bones at all, Lexi fell forward on her elbows, chest heaving and ass up in the air. So fucking sexy, but he shouldn't have done this. Not as a reaction to Robbie. She deserved better.

With a slick sound, Ryder pulled his dick out of her. "I'm sorry," he murmured. Fuckin' failure.

"What for?" she asked, confusion tainting her pretty voice.

Ryder grabbed his cell phone from where he'd dropped it, snatched his jeans off the floor, and bolted out of the bedroom.

"Ryder!" Lexi called. Her bare footsteps sounded hollowly on the floorboards behind him, but she wasn't fast like him. She wasn't a freak like him.

He bolted for the woods and then hid in the

shadows. He hated himself as he watched her cry on the front porch. He wanted to rip his hair out and scream as the flashbacks pummeled him again. Robbie was supposed to care for him more than anyone in the world, but he'd broken him instead. Not just once or twice, but systematically for years. Pain made up his first memory. Fucking Robbie and fucking shifter healing that allowed that prick to hurt him as much as he wanted.

He should've told mom. She would've killed him, and then Robbie wouldn't be scratching at the locked safe of nightmare memories. Or he should've told Mason. Mason would've split Robbie from dick to throat and pissed on his intestines, but abuse didn't work like that. The physical part hurt, but the mental part was even worse. Abusers knew how to make their victims think the pain was their own goddamned fault. If Ryder had only been good enough, or human enough, Robbie wouldn't have had to hurt him. Blah, blah, fuckin' blah. Robbie's apologies afterward were always the same. Non-existent or blaming Ryder for not being a better kid.

Fuckin' little freak, you better not tell your mom. Little pussy. Are you still crying? God! Sometimes I really hate you.

He used to lock him in a dark closet afterward so Ryder could think about what he'd done. It was a cop-out. Robbie was just hiding his bruises and cuts and broken pieces from the world. Ryder had been scared of the dark, but did Robbie give a fuck about that? No. He reveled in Ryder's crying. Told him over and over it was time to "man up." Five fucking years old, and he needed to man up after being beaten?

Ryder remembered Robbie fighting his mom hard to get time with him, but then he would leave him for days with Ryder's grandparents. And when he did show up, his temper was like dynamite, the fuse already lit and half-burned up. If Ryder wasn't the perfect little pretend-human in every way, he got shattered. Ryder would Change into his owl out of terror, and it would make his real dad even madder. Robbie was openly anti-shifter and so ashamed of Ryder's inner owlet.

Ima beat that animal right out of you.

Five fucking years old, and Ryder had twenty memories of abuse to conjure in flashbacks. Stupid fucking mind for being like a steel trap, clinging to all the goddamn horrors. *He was supposed to love me!*

Ryder clutched the back of his head and wished to God he could cut that part of his brain out of his skull.

In the porchlight, Lexi wiped her damp cheeks and went back inside, closed the door behind her with a soft *click*. Good, at least she was safe, and now he could get ahold of himself the only way he could think of. Ryder strode along the edge of the woods until he reached his cabin up the hill, and then he bolted up the ladder and sat down on the roof like he and Clinton used to do when the world got too fucking heavy to shoulder. Spinning the phone end over end between his fingers, Ryder stared at the blue half-moon surrounded by all her stars.

Ryder hit the speed dial for home. Two rings and then, "Boy, you okay?"

At the sound of Mason's voice, Ryder wanted to curl up in a ball and cry like a fucking baby.

"No," he said, his voice breaking on the word.

"You want your momma to hear?"

Ryder shook his head like Mason could see it, swallowed hard, and forced the answer past his tightened vocal chords. "No."

"Hang on, I'm headed to the roof."

A minute of static on the line later, and Mason

said, "Boy, tell me you can see that moon."

"I'm looking at it right now." The same one, and somehow that made him feel better, like he wasn't so far away from the man who should've been his real, biological father.

"Tell me." Mason's voice was deep and sleepy, somber.

"Robbie sent me a message."

"Fuck." A rasping sound came through like Mason was rubbing his hand over and over his beard. "Fuckin' mother fucking fucker."

Ryder huffed a hollow laugh. "Yep, that's about right."

"Tell me what it said."

And he did. Ryder repeated the messages word-for-word from memory because apparently his mind was broken enough to cling tight to the shit that hurt him the most.

"You know, I told him this would happen. I called it. I told him not to give up his rights because he would regret it someday and come crawling back, and look what happened. I want to kill him. Not because I'm jealous he's your real dad, but because he's a fuckin' asshole. Messin' with your head like this," Mason grumbled. "Well good. I'm glad he's dyin'. I hope it's going slow for him. What are you gonna do?"

Feeling completely lost, Ryder shook his head for a long time. "I met a girl."

Mason was quiet for the span of three breaths before he murmured, "*The* girl?"

"I think so. I get heat in my chest around her, and she makes me want to fix all the bad shit in my head just to be good enough for her."

"And now Robbie comes along."

"Exactly. Terrible timing." Ryder was tempted to tell him everything. Every awful memory Robbie had given him, but what good would that do now? It would only make Mason and Mom think they'd messed up somewhere along the line and been unapproachable. It wasn't like that. Robbie had just convinced Ryder that if he tattled, he was weak and would always be weak. And he'd so badly wanted to be strong like Mason and the other Boarlanders he'd grown up idolizing. "I can't think of a single reason why I should see him. Nothing he could possibly say would change things. I don't want to spiral, you know? I'm just getting my life together, and I don't want Robbie to hurt Lexi in any way. And I just get this awful feeling deep down in my gut that the backlash would trickle through me and into her."

"And it would, especially if you're bonded."

"I don't know if we're bonded. I've thought that a dozen times before, and I wasn't."

"You got heat in your chest around her. That's a good sign."

It could also be a good sign Ryder was just desperate to see signs where there weren't any, and he was determined to take things as slow as Lexi needed.

"Ryder, you know I have to tell your mom, right? I tell her everything. She should know Robbie's trying to get back in your life."

"Yeah, I know."

"Will you call us tomorrow and let us know how you're holding up?"

"Sure."

Mason let off an explosive exhale. "Ryder, you've always made me so fuckin' proud. Anytime I was out with you in public and someone commented on you behaving, or being cute, or complimented my beautiful family, well I just puffed up a like a proud rooster. And then I got to watch you grow into this funny, loyal, good man, and I get cocky about it, like I had somethin' to do with you growin' up right. But it's you. You're strong like your momma. I'm sorry for what Robbie's done. I always hated it, but I'm glad I got a shot at being your step-dad."

Ryder swallowed over and over to make sure his voice would come out steady. "Mason, Robbie's just Robbie." His eyes burned, and he scrubbed his hand down his face. "You're my real dad."

Mason sounded all choked up when he said, "I love you, boy."

Ryder wiped his damp cheek on his shoulder and murmured, "Love you, too."

And after they hung up, Ryder responded to Robbie's message.

You have the wrong number.

Ryder wasn't the son of some abusive, prejudiced, dead-beat asshole.

He got lucky enough to be the son of the most honorable man he'd ever met.

Fuck Robbie.

Ryder was the son of Beast Boar.

THIRTEEN

Lexi wrung her hands over and over from her place on the couch as she stared directly at the front door. Even if it took him all night to come back, she would be here waiting.

Something was wrong with Ryder.

There was some deep ache inside of him that he was trying to soothe. She hadn't realized it when he'd come at her like an animal earlier. She'd just recognized he wanted her and got lost in the moment because she loved him wild.

But the sick look on his face when they'd finished pierced her heart.

He'd bolted, but she wasn't angry. She was worried.

His eyes—they'd never looked so bottomless and hollow. And his smile lines had disappeared like they'd never existed at all. It was as if he'd seen a ghost.

The door creaked open, and Ryder cast her a quick glance, then away. She didn't miss it though—the shame there.

His voice cracked when he said, "I'm sorry I left like that."

He stood there, gaze averted to the floor, shoulders hunched like he had a thousand pounds resting on them. His jeans were folded neatly and draped over his arm. Perhaps he'd Changed and hadn't bothered to dress again.

"Can you come here?" she asked gently.

Ryder ran his palm roughly from the back of his hair to the front, mussing his fiery hair. He clenched his jaw so hard a muscle twitched under his eye, but he gave in and sat beside her.

"What happened?"

The air grew heavier, harder to breathe. "I know you want answers, but I need a little time."

His rejection hurt. "Why won't you just let me in?"

"Because I don't want you to see this part of me. Not yet. It's not something I've shared with anyone, and I've only had you one week, Lexi. I want more before you run."

"I'm not running, so—"

"You will if you see how fucked up everything gets in my head. I'm working on being good enough for you—"

"You are good enough—"

"No, I'm not! Not yet. I will be. I swear it. I'll work hard and get through my shit, but I want to tell you everything when I won't break down like a fucking baby in front of you. Okay?"

"Give me something, Ryder. Please."

Ryder grimaced, baring his teeth for a moment before he composed his face and poked a couple buttons on his cell phone. He handed it to her and then stood and strode for the bedroom, leaving her to read the damning messages alone.

His real dad was back, messaging him after twenty-five years of rejection and silence. After abandoning him and signing away all his parental rights. And as she read Ryder's simple, clipped response, *You have the wrong number*, she knew his story was much deeper than he'd told her, or anyone else.

His real dad was dying, and still, Ryder wanted nothing to do with him.

Lexi clutched the phone to her chest, and something white caught her attention.

On her lap sat Ryder's apology, a promise that he was still here. There sat his pledge that he was trying. He couldn't give her all the answers yet, but he'd given her the piece of himself he was able.

On her lap sat a long, snow-white feather.

FOURTEEN

"Sexy Lexi, tell me you're off work."

Lexi giggled over the phone, but it was barely audible over all the raucous in the background. "Sorry, lover. I'll have to join you boys later. I've got a bachelor party, and they hired me for a few extra hours to play bartender and make snacks. At least it's in the big cabin! Plus they are tipping like crazy."

Something big shattered in the background, and Ryder winced away from the phone. "What the hell was that?"

"Oh my gosh, I have to go. Someone just knocked over a vase. I love you. I love you! Don't get drunk until I get there! Oh, and Ryder?"

"Yeah, babe?"

"Congratulations. I'm so fucking proud of you! Tell Wes hi. Okay, gotta go." She made a couple of smacking kiss noises into the phone, and then the line went dead.

Bachelor parties were now Ryder's least favorite part of Lexi's job. She was a professional personal chef, not a beer wench for drunken, sloppy wanker-faces.

Wes sat down at the bar beside him and ordered them a couple of beers from Bubba, Drat's Boozehouse's newest bartender.

"Is Lexi stuck at work?" Wes asked.

"Yeah, she'll be here when she can."

A lot had happened over the last week. A major push from Ryder and Wes had the Big Flight ATV Tours building almost finished, and today they'd booked their first paid tour, happening one month from today. With the deposit, the business was officially up and running and cause for celebration. Nine o'clock was still early to go hard at the shots, but Wes had wanted to meet up for dinner, just the two of them, like a fucking bro-date. He would have given him some major shit if he didn't find it so cute. Wes played like he was hard, but ever since they were kids, he'd always made sure they got one-on-one blood brother time. The little stage-five clinger. Ryder hooked his arm around the back of his neck and ran his knuckles roughly over Wes's dark hair.

"Get off, asshole," Wes muttered, shoving him hard. He rubbed a hand over his hair and grumbled, "Man, that's why I like wearing a baseball cap around you. Fuckin' knuckle sandwiches, really? You're like a child in a man's body."

"You looooove me," Ryder sang, then took a long swig of beer and waggled his eyebrows once at Wes over the bottle.

"Speaking of loooooving someone, how are you and Lexi doing?"

"Fucking awesome, I want to marry her and put a dozen owl babies in her."

Wes's face went completely slack, and he jerked his gaze away.

"What?"

"Nothing," Wes said too fast.

Fuckin' little fucker. "Tell me!"

Wes opened his mouth, then clacked his teeth closed, took a long drink of his beer, stalling like a pro. Ryder was a patient hunter, though, so he let him down his whole stupid beer.

Bubba set the burger baskets Ryder had ordered for them on the bar, but the second Wes reached for a fry, Ryder yanked the food away from him.

"What the hell?" Wes asked.

"Tell me what that look was for, or no food for you."

"Come on, man." Wes reached for his basket, but Ryder snatched it away and licked one of the burgers.

Ryder stuck his tongue out right above the other one and made his eyes as big as he could. "I'll thuckin' do ith," he swore around his tongue.

"Lexi told Alana about what happened last week, and Alana told me."

Ryder frowned and tossed Weston's un-licked food to him. Four fries fell off the side. "I don't know what you're talking about and furthermore, Alana is being a terrible second best friend."

"She's worried about you, so that would make her an awesome second best friend. She asked me to talk to you, but I already know you're a horrible sharer, so I just wanted you to know if you need to talk…you can talk to me, and I probably won't make fun of you."

"Noted, now what was that look really for? Because I know it wasn't for that bullshit."

"Nope, that was it." But Wessy-poo wouldn't meet his eyes, and now the Novak Raven was very busy stuffing his face with his burger.

Ryder didn't buy it, but whatever. He had beers to drink and onion rings to devour and pussy to lick, because he was gonna *get* Lexi's tasty little morsel tonight. His dick thumped against the seam of his jeans just thinking about her writhing under his mouth, gripping his hair, pulling him closer, begging shamelessly, screaming his name. His mate was a noisy little critter.

"Why are you smiling like that?" Wes asked through a grossed-out grimace.

Ryder took a giant bite of burger and nodded to the dark-headed loner at the end of the bar. With a gulp, Ryder jerked his head in invitation and said, "Kane, come be social."

"Hard pass." The Blackwing Dragon hadn't even taken his eyes off the soccer game on the television screen behind the bar when he answered.

Ryder groaned. "Kaaaane. Just fucking do it so I don't have to move all my stuff down there."

Kane slammed the rest of his drink and twitched his head at Bubba, ordering another. With a muttered curse that started with "M" and ended with "other fucker," Kane plopped down onto the stool beside Ryder and jacked up his black eyebrows behind his sunglasses. "Happy?"

"Yes, thank you for asking. I'm now getting laid once a night—"

"I don't care."

"—and our business is taking off—"

"Still don't care."

"—and yesterday, I convinced my mate to wear a thong for a whole hour—"

"Don't caaaare."

"—and now I've got a Blackwing Dragon as my fourth best friend."

Kane looked sad and defeated. God, Ryder loved annoying people. Beside him, Wes snickered and shook his head.

"S'cuse me, Ryder Anderson?" a man asked from behind them.

Ryder glanced over his shoulder at a grizzly-looking older man with a long, scruffy beard and silver, greasy hair. His skin was leathered, his wrinkles deep, but there was a hardness in his dark eyes that had Ryder's hackles on the rise.

Wes murmured, "His last name's Croy, and he's eating, man. He can sign autographs after we're done." His tone sounded as troubled as Ryder felt.

Ryder forced himself to turn his back on the predator. He didn't smell like a shifter. Wes and Kane were still staring at the man behind him and would keep his exposed side safe enough, but fuck, he wanted away from this guy.

"You know me."

"I assure you I don't."

"You don't recognize me, son?"

Ryder's heart dropped to the toes of his boots. Robbie Anderson. He blinked slowly and stared at the liquor case behind the bar, wishing he could smash one of them across the asshole's cheekbone.

Ryder offered the old man his profile, then glared at him over his shoulder. "What the fuck do you want?"

"You ignored my messages."

"I think you should leave," Wes said coolly. The air reeked of dominance and anger now. Wes had seen all the bad years. He'd witnessed the aftermath of Robbie's destruction.

"Two minutes of your time is all I'm beggin'." There was still a hardness that didn't match his pleading words, and all Ryder wanted to do was escape. He wanted to tuck Lexi under his wing and move away, break his bond to the Bloodrunners, hide for the rest of his life in a hole deep enough that Robbie would never find him again.

"Two minutes, and you'll never have to see me again."

Ryder turned slowly on the barstool. As he locked gazes with the man, the slight familiarity was there. It was in the eyes. They hadn't softened in all these years. "I want your word on that. I mean, your word's pretty fuckin' flimsy, but I want it anyway."

"You have my word." Robbie's lips twisted into an empty smile, as if pretending he wasn't a snake.

Ryder followed him to a booth nearby, all the while thanking the powers that be that Lexi was working late and not here to witness this. When the old man's face melded with the cruel face that had laughed when five-year-old Ryder had been lying on the floor, clutching his throbbing cheek, Ryder's heartrate went crazy. He clenched his fists against the urge to strangle the final breaths out of Robbie right here and now. Ryder tossed a look back at Wes, whose eyes had gone black as a raven's, and Kane was staring after him with an unreadable gaze behind those sunglasses.

And for a moment, Ryder felt like a child again, sent off by his mom to spend a few days with Robbie. The fear was still there. But as Ryder sat back on the booth seat, he studied the monster who had been lurking in the shadows of his life all this time, and he came to realize something. Robbie Anderson was just a man, not a monster. He only had the power Ryder gave him, and that shit ended now.

Ryder wasn't some scared kid anymore. He wasn't small and helpless. He had fifty pounds of muscle on his biological father, more fighting experience under his belt than humans could guess at, and his owl wasn't the terrified, gray, little owlet anymore. Inside, his animal raged to be set free to bleed this man.

Robbie made a disgusted ticking sound and said, "Nice eyes." *Fuckin' little freak.*

Ryder wanted to pummel his face with his bare hands. "Two minutes. What do you want?"

"I came to see how much you're like me now. I want to go knowing I left my mark on the world."

Ryder huffed a breath and shook his head. "Zero percent like you. I was raised by a good man."

"Raised by one don't mean you're his, boy."

"Don't call me that."

"Why not?"

"Because my real dad calls me that. He earned nicknames. You earned nothing."

"*I'm* your real dad. My blood runs through your veins, Ryder. I *named* you. I watched you come screaming into this world, and no dad was prouder."

"Bullshit." Ryder shook his head, disgusted. He looked around the bar, anywhere but at Robbie's dead eyes.

"You feel the emptiness yet?"

Bile clawed up the back of Ryder's throat as he crossed his arms.

"You feel the hole? The one you can't fill up with anything. That's from me. That's from your granddad and great granddad, down through the generations. And oh, I was just like you, thinkin' I would break the curse. It's why I tried so hard with your mom."

"You didn't try. I remember everything. I

remember how unhappy you made her. How you didn't want to touch her. I saw you standing on the other side of her bedroom door when she was sobbing one night, and you were smiling. You were a shit husband."

"I did the best I could with her, and you'll do the same to the woman you play house with. Why do you think you're thirty and still haven't settled down? I used to hate the curse. Hated being the way I was, until I didn't anymore. One day I just realized some men are made for families, and some men are made for procreation. We Anderson's are made for the latter."

Ryder hated him. Hated him for what he was doing. Consciously, Ryder knew this was horseshit. His dad was just a lowlife abusive sonofabitch. He was a master manipulator who could turn words and phrases and make people question everything. He was that good at lying. But right now, his words made so much damn sense. Maybe Beaston and Weston never saw him with a mate because he had that poisonous Anderson blood flowing through his veins. Maybe he'd been broken from birth.

Robbie leaned forward. "The best thing you can

do is leave your baby mommas to raise your mistakes, because I see the monster in you, Ryder. It's the same monster that lives in me."

"I remember what you did," Ryder gritted out. "I remember everything. Every bruise, every scratch, every fractured bone, every drop of blood. I remember every hateful word you spewed at me, and I remember how you would look my mom in her eyes and tell her you took good care of me when she wasn't around, you piece of shit. Damn straight you got a monster in you, Robbie. But I'm nothing like you. Two minutes is up. Do the world a favor and die quickly."

Ryder stood, but Robbie followed him toward the bar. "I wanted a different life for you. Your mom and that boar ruined you. I only made girls after you, and my only son who coulda carried on my family name was brainwashed with all that hippy-dippy shifter shit."

"Yeah, well that shifter shit is my life since I'm a fuckin' shifter and all."

"You weren't supposed to be!"

Rage blasted through Ryder's body, and the edges of his vision collapsed inward. In an instant, he had Robbie against the back wall, his hand crushing his throat. "What do you mean by that?"

"I tried to save you."

"Save me from what?"

"From that fucking animal your momma put inside of you."

The feel of Robbie's sagging, clammy skin made Ryder sick. He released him and stared at the old man in horror. "What did you do?"

"I signed you up for a program that would've given you a normal life, and your mom said no. I fought hard for you, but that asshole boar pushed me out of your life."

"What program?" Ryder asked low. It better not be what he fucking thought it was.

"You would've been one of the first to be genetically cleansed."

Ryder linked his hands behind his head and backed up a couple of steps. He wanted to retch at what Robbie had admitted. Mom and Mason hadn't ever told him this. Why the fuck hadn't they told him? *Because it would hurt you worse. They were protecting you.*

Ryder hated Robbie. Hated. Him.

In a ragged whisper, he asked, "You wanted to torture me? You wanted to strip my animal away? Why? Because I wasn't like you? Because I wasn't human enough? You fucking asshole. You arrogant fucking asshole. You aren't top of the food chain! I am! Genetic cleansing, are you fucking kidding me? That's why you gave up parental rights, isn't it?" Ryder wrenched his voice louder. "Isn't it?"

"Of course it is! I had to make a stand, and I wasn't raising some little fr—"

Ryder hit him across the jaw to stop that word from tumbling past his lips. "Don't you fucking say it."

Hunched to the side, Robbie spat red and favored his swollen lip when he said, "Genetic cleansing would've fixed you."

Ryder was shoved backward, and his view of Robbie was blocked by Kane's massive shoulders. The Blackwing Dragon pushed Robbie up the wall, locking his arm across Robbie's throat.

Robbie was red and choking, gagging, clawing at Kane's arm. Ryder stood with his hands out, wondering what the fuck was happening.

"You think genetic cleansing fixes shifters?" Kane growled out in a terrifying voice. "It doesn't fix shit."

He tossed Robbie like a ragdoll across the room and limped after him unrushed. Smoothly, Kane bent down and pulled a knife from where it had been hidden near his ankle.

"Kane!" Wes warned, but the Blackwing Dragon didn't even hesitate. His limp eased with each step until he walked smooth as a predator.

Robbie was scrambling backward on the floor, terror written on his face. How utterly satisfying to watch his dad scared of pain.

Wes put himself between Kane and Robbie, but Kane shoved the Novak Raven out of the way like he was nothing.

"Ryder!" Wes yelled.

Fuck, Wes was right. As much as Robbie deserved to die, Kane would be locked up for murder. And not in a regular prison. He would be caged where they hid the dangerous shifters from the world.

Ryder bolted for him and cut him off. "Man, don't do this. He isn't worth it."

But Kane's sunglasses had come off, and his green dragon eyes were glowing and fixed on Robbie. He didn't even see Ryder. This wasn't Kane anymore. This was a peek at that destructive Blackwing blood that ran through him. This was a glimpse at Dark Kane.

Ryder pushed him hard, and Wes went at him, too, pushing, pushing, losing ground. The last thing they needed was Kane murdering a human in front of all these witnesses. Or worse yet, losing all control and shifting. One dragon shift in tight quarters, and everyone in here would die. There were others helping now, humans, bar patrons, trying to slow Kane down, and Bubba was dragging Robbie behind the bar.

Kane surged forward, and in desperation to save him, Ryder hit him hard, over and over across his stony jaw until his hand shattered. Pain blasted through his arm. "Snap out of it, Kane!"

"This isn't even fucking worth it!" Robbie yelled. "You all saw this. He tried to kill me. No amount of money is worth this bullshit."

"What do you mean no amount of money?" Ryder yelled.

"I ain't here to apologize, you fuckin' freak. I'm here because I'm getting paid!" he crowed through a bloody smile. "They're comin' for you, boy, because you're weak. Weak, weak, weak, just like I always knew you would be." Bubba was shoving him hard toward the door.

Ryder held his throbbing hand to his stomach, gave up on trying to hold Kane back since Robbie was getting bullied toward the exit. The struggling crowd behind him bumped Ryder hard in the back, and he stumbled two steps forward. "Who's paying you?"

"Hunting like a pack, going after the lowest ranking member of the crew first, which is my boy. What a fuckin' surprise!"

"Who?" Ryder roared.

Right before Robbie disappeared out the exit door, he offered Ryder a vile grin and said, "Wolves got your girl."

FIFTEEN

Lexi poured one last line of shots and screwed the cap back on the whiskey as the groom-to-be, Axton, made a toast.

"To Lexi, who is sweet as honey and easy on the eyes. To Lexi, who has given us all something to look forward to."

That toast was weird, but they were all drunk, so okay.

She smiled politely and lifted her water bottle as the boys howled and cheered. Axton stared at her too long before he drank his shot down. He was tall and lithe with a runner's body. He wore a thick, dark beard, but it didn't cover the scar on the side of his face completely. These men seemed like a rough and tumble group, so maybe he got that in a rock climbing accident or a motorcycle crash or something. His eyes were a striking gray color that probably drove his fiancé wild. Gold was more of Lexi's color, though.

Uncomfortable with yet another direct stare from Axton, she busied herself with cleaning up and readying to leave. The men, all mid-twenties to early thirties were good tippers. She wouldn't have stayed if they weren't and, for the most part, they had been respectful enough. None had touched her or said anything inappropriate.

It was the way they looked at her that made her skin crawl, though. And there was some spark of excitement in the air that she didn't understand.

"Lexi, I thank you kindly for feeding my boys and me," Axton said in a conversational tone from across the kitchen island. "I don't think we'll be needing your services anymore tonight."

Some of the men around him made strange whooping sounds, as if excited for her to leave. Weird.

"Sounds good. Thank you all for being such a fun crowd, and I wish you big luck on your upcoming wedding."

Axton dropped his head and huffed a laugh, and when he lifted his chin again, his eyes looked lighter, more mercury silver than gray. "I ain't the marrying kind, but I thank you for the well-wishes."

"Oh." She frowned, utterly baffled. "But you said this was a bachelor party."

"Well..." He looked at the men gathering around him. "We're a bunch of bachelors, and this *is* a party."

"More like a war party, though," one of the shorter men said. His dark eyes had lightened to a caramel brown that seemed to glow, and now Lexi's fine hairs were rising all over her body.

"Great," she said, ducking her gaze and pretending she didn't see the changes happening here. These men weren't human. This was some kind of crew function that she'd unknowingly been hired to serve.

She grabbed the pile of tips from the counter and folded the bills into her pocket, then shouldered her tote she'd brought with her. Half of her things were still on the counter, but fuck it. She could come back for them later. Right now, all she wanted to do was get out of here.

"Bloodrunner whore." A tall man with tattoos all

over his neck spat on the floor right where she was about to step.

Lexi gasped and stumbled over the puddle of spittle. Clutching her tote bag tightly, she walked faster toward the door. She had a set of good knives, and she would use them if pushed. When she cast a glance over her shoulder, all the men with matching, feral smiles were following her slowly.

Oh God, she just needed to get to her Jeep. Lexi threw open the door and bolted across the porch, past the bubbling hot tub, and down the steep stairs as fast as she could. It was dark out, but the lights from the house illuminated the clearing in gold, and the moon above was almost full, casting the surrounding woods in an eerie blue.

Jogging across the lawn toward the corner of the house, she pulled out her biggest knife and her cell phone. Heart galloping in her chest, she dialed Ryder with shaking fingers.

Axton appeared at her side like an apparition, blurring as he ripped the phone from her hand and chucked it at a tree. It shattered into a thousand pieces against the bark, and on reflex, Lexi slashed with her blade, catching him down the arm.

Axton hissed in pain and held his bleeding arm, but as he looked down at the red streaming through his fingers, he smiled, like he found her amusing. And now his eyes were churning such a light gray, they were almost white.

"Get away from me," she demanded, holding out the blade. Damn her hand as it shook!

Axton's grin turned wolfish as he held his hands up in surrender and let her pass.

Adrenaline pumping through her, Lexi backed toward the gravel parking spot she'd left her Jeep. Some instinct deep inside of her screamed, *don't give him your back*!

But this view was terrifying. Axton's men were following her slowly, too gracefully, all of their eyes glowing in the dark like monsters. They were spreading out slowly, the ends of the line curving toward her, herding her.

When Lexi's shoes hit the line of gravel, she turned to sprint for her Jeep, but what she saw made no sense. Her Wrangler was laying on its side, wheels pointed directly at her.

No. No, no, no, that was her escape!

"We'll let you keep your little knife," Axton said

in a voice that was too low and growly now. "We'll even give you a two-minute head start. Makes the chase more fun that way."

"W-what chase?"

"My pack needs to hunt. We're predators," Axton explained, canting his head like an animal. "You understand?"

"Please. I just want to go home."

One of the men wrenched his voice up an octave and repeated, "Please!"

"Please let me go home," another taunted her.

Axton pointed through the woods with a bloody finger. "That way is the main road. Reach the asphalt, and we'll let you live."

"I don't trust you."

"Probably wise. Werewolves aren't known for their trustworthiness, but what choice do you have?"

Behind him, bones snapped and men hunched over. Snarling, growling beasts burst from his pack one-by-one, each twice the size of a regular wolf with bloodlust glowing in their eyes.

Lexi couldn't breathe from the terror that settled into her chest. She backed up, shaking her head in denial. This couldn't be happening. It couldn't!

Her back hit the undercarriage of her jeep, and she whimpered, clutching her knife in a white-knuckled grip.

Axton's face was elongating, his frost-colored eyes locked on her as his bones broke and his muscles reshaped gruesomely. And right before he morphed into a black-furred wolf, he fell to his hands and knees and snarled out, "Run, little bunny."

With a gasp of horror, she bolted around the Jeep and looked around the back of the house for their cars. They had to drive here, right? But even if she spent the time to find them, would the keys be inside? Probably not, and then she would've wasted her two-minute head start.

She didn't have time for the tears that blurred her vision as she sprinted for the dirt road that would lead her to safety. Tears would slow her down, and she needed to keep her head, not fall apart right now.

She had to reach the asphalt of the main road.

Think!

Lexi dropped the tote bag and stripped out of her white chef coat. She wore a navy tank top and black skinny jeans underneath. They would still smell her easily enough. Hell, she was probably leaving a trail of fear-scent behind her, but at least she wouldn't be a fucking beacon in the white coat.

Behind her, the howl of a wolf rose on the wind, followed by another and another. God, if she could've just gotten the call into Ryder sooner, or even if it had rung once, her number would've flashed across his caller ID, and he would've known she needed something. Now, no one would know she was in trouble until it was too late. Until she was cold and lifeless in these woods.

The image of him mourning her burst against her mind. Fuck. She couldn't' leave him like this. He'd been hurt enough.

Don't think like that. Just run. Fight. Live. Be strong.

Lexi pushed her legs faster as she bolted down the even ground of the dirt road that would lead her to the main turnoff. The wolves would find her easily here, but if she cut into the woods too soon, she faced the possibility of getting turned around or lost.

The knife flashed in her hand every time she pumped her arms, and it settled her fractionally. At least she wasn't weaponless. At lease she could take one of the wolves with her.

Go for the throat, not the ribs. Cut arteries in the neck, render the esophagus helpless.

Her legs burned, and her lungs felt like they would burst. There was movement to her right in the woods. It was a lone, white wolf, keeping pace with her and cutting in gently. Shit. Had it already been two minutes? They were so fast!

Panicked, Lexi swerved into the woods on her left and cut an angle due north toward the road. The ground was uneven and harder to run on. One twisted ankle, and she would be done for. Howling came from her right, and now there were two wolves, the white one and a dark gray one. More pressure, and she was veering off course. What choice did she have? They were too close.

She skidded down a hill on her butt, hand out behind her to steady her from toppling over as she dislodged dirt and leaves on the way down. She knew where she was—the creek. If she went straight across and kept the moon on her left, she could still make it to the road.

As she reached the creek bank, pain slashed through her palm as she cut it on a rock. "Fuck," she gasped out breathlessly, clenching her hand into a fist to staunch the immediate wet stream. If they couldn't smell her before, they sure as hell would be drawn by the blood. Another wolf song lifted on the breeze, this time on her left. They were closing on her, and she had to move.

Lexi pushed upward and ran straight into the creek. It was flowing steadily because of the spring rains, and when she reached the middle, she sank in to her hips. Frantically dragging her legs through the current, she plunged her injured hand into the cold water and hoped it helped.

Lexi yanked her shirt over her head, then wrapped the tank around her hand and gripped it hard to hold it in place. Wincing at the pain, she clutched her knife tighter and sprinted through the woods. The terrain eased into an incline, and she huffed and puffed as she climbed higher and higher. She didn't recognize this area anymore, but there were three wolves on her right. And to her horror, there were now three on her left loping beside her through the blue trees, snapping at each other, snarling, waiting for something Lexi didn't understand. She was completely trapped into moving wherever they wanted her to. Seconds stretched to minutes, and it felt as if she was in a dream. One where she ran and ran and never escaped the shadows that were chasing her. Terror pushed her on, even when her body wanted to give out. Even when her legs shook and her stomach heaved. The incline evened out, but she could hear them. She could feel them right behind her. Any second the wolves would be on her. Their teeth would be shredding her flesh, and she would die on her stomach, alone.

Ryder, Ryder, Ryder.

She almost didn't see the ledge until it was too late. Lexi locked her legs and skidded on the loose dirt. She spun and went to her hands, clawing desperately on the dirt to stop herself. Her foot slid off the side, and she grunted in panic as she scrambled back onto solid ground. A rock dislodged under her and tumbled down. She listened in horror for the rock to hit the ground below with a resounding crash. Seven seconds.

That's when it hit her—what the wolves had done.

The road was so close, less than a quarter of a mile due north, but separated from her by this ravine.

The wolves had hunted her as a pack, pushing her and maneuvering her until the road wasn't possible to reach. Until there was no way she could win this game. She hadn't ever really had a chance. Rage and fear boiled in her middle as a massive black wolf approached.

She moved to run to the side, but the white and gray wolf were there, teeth bared and glowing against the shadows. On the other side, there were four more wolfs, stalking closer, heads lowered, razor sharp teeth promising a painful death.

Axton lifted his chin and perked his ears like he was proud of what he was doing. Like he was proud he'd hunted her down and won. Proud murderer.

Lexi spat at him. "You're a coward."

Axton's eyes narrowed to slits, and he lowered his head, eased backward on those massive paws of his like he was giving his pack a gift. The gift of flesh. The gift of killing. He and his people were mindless psychos who had convinced themselves killing was just what predators did. But she knew bigger predator shifters than them, and the Bloodrunners would never disrespect human life like this.

The wolves snapped and snarled, but Lexi

couldn't go out like this. Not under their teeth. Oh, she knew what the bite of a werewolf would do to her. She would be Turned in the last moments of her life, and she would be damned if she died a member of Axton's pack.

She would die human, and fuck the werewolf games.

Lexi gripped the bloody shirt to her chest, breath shaking in terror. The air smelled of pennies. The wolves went mad, snapping, ducking forward and back. There was pack dynamics she didn't understand. A feeding order maybe. Didn't matter now.

Biting her lip against the whimper of fear that clawed up the back of her throat, Lexi stepped backward. The wolves lifted their heads in unison, ears erect, confusion in their eyes.

God, she didn't want to die, but it was coming either way. Knife out, she took another step back, and her heel brushed the ledge. The wind whipped against her bare back, as if Mother Nature was trying to keep her upright.

"No blood for you," she said in a shaky voice. "You lose."

As the gray wolf leapt at her, his eyes deranged, his lips curled back to expose all those razor sharp teeth, Lexi launched herself backward off the ledge.

At least she was taking one of them her.

Just as she fell and the ledge promised to hide her view of the chaos, something massive and black barreled down from the sky and blasted into the gray wolf an instant before the animal hit her in the chest. Her attacker was knocked sideways and away from her, his mouth open and shocked as a high-pitched cry screeched from his throat.

Wait, wait, wait, was that Wes?

If Wes was here, then...

"Ryder!" she screamed when she caught a glimpse of the snowy owl above her, his enormous wingspan blocking out the moon.

He pulled his wings to his sides and dove for her, but she was falling too fast. She struggled against the destiny that was coming for her. Struggled against her death. She could see him so clearly, every feather on his face whipping in the wind, every black speck that decorated his snow white feathers. His gold eyes were like two glowing suns in his face as he tucked his wings tighter against his body.

Seven seconds. That's all she had, and it was almost up.

Tears burned her eyes, but she had to be strong because he wasn't going to reach her. She hoped he would pull up in time and save himself. He should hear what was in her heart before he lost her. He should see she accepted her fate so it would be easier on him.

"Ryder," she choked out as the wind in the trees below kicked up. "I love you."

And then she squeezed her eyes closed and braced herself for the pain.

And it…was…*horrible*. But not the pain she expected. Her arm felt like it was ripped from its socket and shredded by razors. She screamed at the dizzying, excruciating pain as she was jerked in a different direction. Ryder had one of her arms but his grip was off and his long, curved talons had raked up her forearm with the force of his desperate pull.

The outsides of her vision collapsed inward as sparks flew this way and that. She couldn't breathe. It was as if the oxygen had been sucked from her lungs, and now something massive sat on her chest.

She tried to focus on the stars to keep from

passing out, but something had blocked the sky, and everything was dark. An earth-shattering roar shook the mountains, but Lexi still couldn't force a single molecule of air into her lungs, and the pressure and pain were too great.

Fire streaked across the cliff, illuminating the fearsome face of a beastly dragon, and blistering heat blasted against Lexi's skin.

And then everything went dark.

SIXTEEN

Lexi rolled over in her sleep, but flinched away from the slashing pain in her arm. She bolted upright, clutching it across her chest, as if that would stop the burning.

Heart pounding, she looked around the dim room, lit only by the soft glow of the bathroom. She was in ten-ten, and her arm was wrapped up like a mummy limb.

Harper was sitting next to her on the bed with her knees drawn up to her chest and a hollow look on her face. And in that moment, everything came crashing back down on Lexi. The terror, the exhaustion, the feeling that she would never see Ryder again, and then the pain. So much pain.

"Where's Ryder?" she asked, wanting desperately for him to hold her and tell her everything was all right.

Harper shook her head sadly and whispered, "I don't know. Wes went to look for him."

Lexi's mouth went dry as a desert, and she looked down at her bandaged arm. "Is it bad?"

Harper bit her lip hard, then nodded. "Yeah. You'll be scarred. Weston was raised a Gray Back. He can put anyone back together, but Ryder had to really dig in to pull you up. Wes saved the use of your hand, but…"

"But it looks bad. It's okay. It's okay," Lexi chanted, bobbing her head. "At least I'm alive." Nothing in her wanted to look at her arm or the stitches she could feel pulling at her skin. It still felt like someone had dipped her arm in gunpowder and lit a match, but pain was good. It meant she was still breathing, still here.

"Alana, Aaron, and Wyatt just left. I told them to go get some shut-eye. I thought you would sleep until morning, but I wanted to stay just in case."

Lexi offered her a tremulous smile and settled against the mattress. "What happened, Harper?"

The Bloodrunner alpha picked at a loose thread on the comforter. "Axton and the Valdoro pack made threats when I was trying to settle these mountains. They wanted the land, but the previous owner chose to sell to me. Axton said the vamps would finish us off, but they didn't. We chased the Asheville Coven out of the area a few months back, and I guess the pack's need for revenge flared up again. They targeted Ryder."

"It felt like he targeted me."

"Same thing," Harper murmured. "If you had…" Harper swallowed hard. "If the Valdoro pack ended your life, it would've destroyed Ryder. And Ryder's pain would've echoed through the crew bond and maimed us one by one until we were all sick and ruined. And they didn't just go after you tonight, Lexi. While you were running for your life, Ryder's dad showed up at Drat's, and he just…destroyed Ryder."

Lexi sat up straight. "Oh my gosh, what?"

"Axton apparently paid Robbie to keep Ryder distracted while the wolves took care of you."

"What did he say to him?"

"I think that's something Ryder will have to talk to you about. Wes told me part of it, but I had to stop him. Doesn't feel right taking part of Ryder like that without his permission. He's been hiding a lot of pain for a long time."

"Is he okay?"

Harper cast her a quick glance, her blue dragon eye glowing much brighter than her human brown eye. Slowly, she shook her head. "He saw *the* ghost of his past—the one that's haunted him his whole life. He looked in the face of the devil himself as Robbie told him awful things and admitted to being paid to betray him. To hurt him. To hurt you. And then Ryder watched you fall, Lexi. I'll never forget the look on Ryder's face as he watched Wes stitch up your arm where he'd hurt you. He needs time."

She understood, really she did, but it didn't stop the bone-deep desperation to be near him and let him know he wasn't alone.

"What happened to the wolves?" Lexi asked, trying to distract herself from the ripping sensation in her heart.

"Axton and four of his wolves got away."

"And the others?"

Harper's voice went hard as stone when she answered. "I burned them to nothing and devoured their ashes."

Lexi's heart thumped against her sternum as she remembered how terrifying Harper's roaring, fire-breathing dragon was when she'd come to help save her. She was just now realizing how dangerous the steady-voiced woman beside her really was.

Harper leveled her oddly-colored gaze on Lexi and promised, "I'll do the same to anyone who ever tries to hurt you again, okay?"

Lexi nodded and whispered, "Okay." Dangerous though she may be, the Bloodrunner Dragon was loyal to her people, and with that last oath, Harper had just declared Lexi a part of her crew and under her protection.

Lexi settled back beside Harper and rested her temple on the Bloodrunner Dragon's shoulder. "Thanks, alpha."

Harper set her cheek gently on top of Lexi's head and huffed a shallow sigh. "Anytime."

SEVENTEEN

The sun peeked over the mountains, casting the horizon in bright orange. Ryder rubbed his hand over and over his three-day beard and thought of Fishing Mornings. Fishing Mornings were when Bash, Clinton, and Mason would take him out to Bear Trap Falls near the trailer park, and they would all watch the sun come up while they waited for fish to bite.

He'd had it good. Not only did he grow up under Mason, but under the other Boarlanders as well. Robbie had shadowed a corner of his heart for way too damn long.

A limb snapped, and Ryder looked back over his shoulder to see Weston making his way up the trail. "How did you find me?" he croaked out in a sleep-deprived voice.

"Your spot ain't as secret as you think." His blood brother sat down on the log beside him, his camouflage baseball cap shielding his eyes from the early morning sunlight. "Did you get any sleep?"

"No. My mind has been going around and around all night. Wondering what if I hadn't gotten to her, you know? I can't get the fear in her eyes out of my mind. You know what she said at the end, right before she was gonna hit the ground?"

"What?"

"She told me she loved me, like she was already forgiving me. Like she was making sure I would know she wasn't mad for not being able to save her."

Wes nodded for a long time, and then carefully he said, "Have you been thinking about what your dad said?"

"You mean about why he gave up his rights? About how he wanted to torture my owl from me? Fuck, we should've let Kane have his dumb ass. Pisses me off."

"Just pisses you off?"

Ryder inhaled deeply. He could tell Wes was worried. Could sense it. Could practically smell it on his skin, but this wasn't the part when he spiraled. "I got closure yesterday."

Wes jerked his dark gaze to Ryder. "Yeah?"

Ryder made a single ticking sound and picked a long blade of wild grass, began shredding it into small pieces. "It's different when you see evil when you're an adult. When I was a kid, I was supposed to listen to him. I was supposed to believe him because he was the adult and I was the child. He had me good and convinced he was a shitty person because I wasn't a good enough son. That stuck with me. Just dug into my brain and sat there like a parasite this whole time. But yesterday, I saw him for what he is."

"A steaming pile of shit?"

Ryder huffed a laugh and nodded. "Yeah."

"Can I tell you something?" Wes asked.

"Anything, brother."

"That bullshit your dad said about you being like him? He's dead wrong. You have this immovable loyalty to the people you care about. It drove me nuts when we came back here and you just accepted Wyatt, accepted his apology just like that." Wes snapped. "But it's also been something I've always admired about you. Once a person makes friends with Air Ryder Croy, they're under your wing for life. You don't give up on people, man. You know who you remind me of?"

Ryder smiled because he thought he already knew the answer. "Who?"

"Mason. You are nothing like that soulless asshole, Ryder. You never were. He couldn't even keep one woman happy his whole life. That ain't your destiny."

Ryder frowned at the stark honesty in Weston's tone. "What do you mean?"

"I mean Lexi is your mate. She always was."

"You've seen her for me?" Hope and confusion swirled around in Ryder's chest as he sat up straighter and stared at his best friend.

"I lied when I told you I stopped having visions. I had a dream about her the night before you met her in that coffee shop."

Ryder's hands were shaking, so he clamped them together to make it look like he was holding his shit together. "What was the dream?"

"It scared me at first. It was zoomed in on you, sitting in the rocking chair in front of ten-ten, clutching your stomach like you'd been shot. You were lookin' down at your hands, and I could see a tear fall. Just one. I thought you were dying, but then you opened up your hands and you were holding this little baby owl. Little gray and white fluff ball with gold eyes just like yours." Wes sniffed and said, "You looked up at me, and you smiled. I mean the real kind, not the one you use to hide your hurt. The *happy* kind. And when I looked down, Lexi was sitting on the ground between your legs, resting her cheek on your thigh, looking up at you like you hung the moon and all the stars."

"Why didn't you tell me?" Ryder croaked, ducking his gaze so Wes wouldn't see how choked up he was.

"Because I tried to change Alana's fate, and I missed. And thank God, because if I would've succeeded, she and Aaron wouldn't be bonded like they are. They wouldn't be getting married. She wouldn't be a Bloodrunner. Wyatt told me once that it wasn't my job to change the future, and he's right. And you were doing so fucking good. You bonded Lexi to you just fine on your own. You didn't need my prophesy, Ryder."

"You think it's a real bond?"

Wes bellowed a single laugh that echoed across the mountains. "Ryder, anyone with eyes can see it's the real bond. You both light up when you're around each other." He rocked away, pulled something from his back pocket, and handed it to Ryder. "Here." A pocket knife rested on his open palm. The polished woodgrain shone in the sunlight. Etched neatly into it was *R + L*. "My dad taught me how to make these when I was a kid, and when I was ten, he told me that someday, I would make one for you."

"R plus L. Ryder and Lexi?" Ryder asked, taking the gift carefully.

Weston gripped his shoulder and shook him slowly. "Now I know what my dad meant. You'll need this." With a slight smile, Wes ruffled his hair and stood, then sauntered back down the trail without another word.

Just as he disappeared completely, another face appeared, looking worried and uncertain. Lexi.

Of course she would find him. She knew him, heart and soul.

She didn't say anything as she approached slowly. Only stepped over the log and stood in front of him, her pretty green eyes worried as she cupped his cheeks. Her arm was still bandaged, and he winced away from the sight of the thin crimson line that had seeped through. He'd done that—hurt his mate.

Lexi slipped her arms around his neck and held him until his body relaxed completely against hers.

"Will you tell me now?" she murmured.

And he did. He unloaded all his secret memories onto her, and she was strong. She didn't flinch, gasp, or cry—not until the end. She stood there, rocking him gently as he told her about the abuse and the shame that his dad made him feel about his inner animal. He told her about his struggles to cope as he was growing up, and about the hole he'd always felt in his middle. The one he hadn't figured out how to fill up yet. He told her about the guilt he'd shouldered all these years for letting Robbie's actions hurt him, while Mason was working so hard to make him feel loved. He told her about yesterday, and about the genetic cleansing Robbie had tried to do.

And when he was finished, he felt so much better.

It wasn't his burden to bear alone anymore. Lexi had come in and offered to shoulder half and, God, his soul was better for it.

"I'm sorry about your arm," he whispered.

"I looked at it," she squeaked out. "Harper said I should so I didn't imagine the worst."

"And?"

She huffed an emotional laugh and eased back, showed him the emerald green in her pretty eyes. They were rimmed with tears. "At first, I was so sad because it's not something I'll ever be able to hide. Not even in my chef uniform. But…" She ran a knuckle over his jaw, feeling his scruff there. "I thought about something."

"What?"

She swallowed hard, pulled the collar of his shirt aside, and brushed a light touch over the scar Mason made all those years ago. "I know you don't bite to claim a mate, but you let Mason cut you to show that you were his family."

Ryder kissed her palm hard, let his lips linger there because he could see where this was going and it made him love her even more.

"So if it's okay…this?" she said, holding up her bandaged arm. "This is my claiming mark from you. You gave it to me saving my life. I know you would've gone right to the ground with me. I saw it in your eyes. You weren't going to give up on me no matter what." Her face crumpled, and tears streaked down her cheeks. "So if you say it's okay, I'm gonna love these scars because they mean I'm yours."

Fuck, oh fuck, oh fuck. He was going to lose it. Ryder swallowed over and over, trying to get ahold of himself. And now the knife he was clutching in his hand made all the damn sense in the world. Wes had known.

Ryder flipped open the blade and handed it to her, hilt first. She frowned down at it, but as he pulled his shirt off, realization washed through her eyes. Cheeks rosy from crying, lips parted in question, long dark hair in waves down her shoulders, her body framed by the sunrise behind her, his mate had never looked more beautiful.

Hand steady, Lexi rested the blade under the mark Mason had made all those years ago. Carefully, she cut into his skin and dragged the blade all the way to the end of his collarbone, like she wanted the scar to be obvious. Like she wanted it to count. Good mate.

Warmth trickled down his chest, and it stung

something fierce, but damn, it felt good to be claimed by her.

Lexi wiped the stained knife on her jeans and then closed it carefully. She sat in Ryder's lap and rested her cheek against his, watching a sunrise he would never forget for as long as he lived.

He wouldn't tell his mate about Weston's prophecy. He wouldn't tell her about their future child, or how fucking happy he was going to make her.

Wes was right. Ryder didn't need prophecies.

He just needed Lexi.

Lexi had been working her magic from the first moment he saw her. She'd been slowly patching the hole in his heart, and now he didn't feel the void at all. Fuck Robbie and everything he'd done. Ryder was the luckiest sonofabitch on the planet to have landed a dad like Mason, the mom he had, the crew he'd grown up in, and the crew he had now.

He was the luckiest to have found a woman who loved all of him, the good and the bad.

Lexi had asked him once for something real, for a feather.

He leaned in and sipped her lips just to remind

her he loved her.

Lexi—his beautiful, sweet, driven, loyal Lexi—had earned every real piece of him.

AIR RYDER

Want more of these characters?

Air Ryder is the third book in a five book series based in Harper's Mountains.

Check out these other books from T. S. Joyce.

Bloodrunner Dragon
(Harper's Mountains, Book 1)

Bloodrunner Bear
(Harper's Mountains, Book 2)

Novak Raven
(Harper's Mountains, Book 4)

Blackwing Dragon
(Harper's Mountains, Book 5)

About the Author

T.S. Joyce is devoted to bringing hot shifter romances to readers. Hungry alpha males are her calling card, and the wilder the men, the more she'll make them pour their hearts out. She werebear swears there'll be no swooning heroines in her books. It takes tough-as-nails women to handle her shifters.

Experienced at handling an alpha male of her own, she lives in a tiny town, outside of a tiny city, and devotes her life to writing big stories. Foodie, wolf whisperer, ninja, thief of tiny bottles of awesome smelling hotel shampoo, nap connoisseur, movie fanatic, and zombie slayer, and most of this bio is true.

Bear Shifters? Check

Smoldering Alpha Hotness? Double Check

Sexy Scenes? Fasten up your girdles, ladies and gents, it's gonna to be a wild ride.

For more information on T. S. Joyce's work,
visit her website at
www.tsjoyce.com

Printed in Great Britain
by Amazon